"Would It Be So Hard To Describe The Way You Feel?"

His throaty whisper penetrated the hazy shroud of pleasure surrounding her.

Samantha drew back a little, reluctant to break away from him, not wanting to disturb the web of enchantment he spun so easily around her. Jason Armstrong was magic. There was magic in his voice, magic in his touch, magic in his words.

"Not for a writer." A soft smile curved her mouth, and this time the disbelief was gone from her tone. "Are you really Cathryn James?"

"In the flesh," he said softly, tipping her face up to his to search her eyes. "Are you disappointed?"

Dear Reader,

Welcome to Silhouette! Our goal is to give you hours of unbeatable reading pleasure, and we hope you'll enjoy each month's six new Silhouette Desires. These sensual, provocative love stories are both believable and compelling—sometimes they're poignant, sometimes humorous, but always enjoyable.

Indulge yourself. Experience all the passion and excitement of falling in love along with our heroine as she meets the irresistible man of her dreams and together they overcome all obstacles in the path to a happy ending.

If this is your first Desire, I hope it'll be the first of many. If you're already a Silhouette Desire reader, thanks for your support! Look for some of your favorite authors in the coming months: Stephanie James, Diana Palmer, Dixie Browning, Ann Major and Doreen Owens Malek, to name just a few.

Happy reading!

Isabel Swift
Senior Editor

SDRL-7/85

SANDRA KLEINSCHMIT
Heaven on Earth

Silhouette Desire

Published by Silhouette Books New York

America's Publisher of Contemporary Romance

SILHOUETTE BOOKS
300 E. 42nd St., New York, N.Y. 10017

Copyright © 1986 by Sandra Kleinschmit

Distributed by Pocket Books

ISBN: 0-373-05255-3

First Silhouette Books printing January 1986

10 9 8 7 6 5 4 3 2 1

America's Publisher of Contemporary Romance

Printed in the U.S.A.

SANDRA KLEINSCHMIT

has been an avid reader all her life, and she's the first to admit that her decision to write romances is based solely on her love of reading romances. She's been writing for nearly three years and still has a difficult time deciding which she enjoys more—writing or reading! Before pursuing a full-time writing career, Sandra worked as a secretary and a military personnel clerk. She lives in Salem, Oregon, with her husband and three daughters.

To Ed,
my husband. . .my hero

One

Samantha Monroe cast a furtive glance in both directions before leaning down to rummage through the yellow canvas bag at her side. Sunglasses, suntan oil, a neatly folded beach towel . . . oh, yes, there it was. A smile of anticipation creased her lips as she lifted the thick paperback from her bag and placed it on her upraised knees. It was no accident that her hands curled around the front cover of the book, her fingers strategically shielding a certain portion of the heroine's rather lush anatomy which was nearly revealed in its entirety. The beach was nearly deserted, but Samantha was taking no chances. Her own eyes had widened considerably when she had spotted the two figures so intimately entwined on the book's cover, but she couldn't resist. Another romance by Cathryn James. It had been on the bestseller list for weeks already, and it was bound to be heaven.

Half an hour later Samantha was oblivious to anything and everything around her, her thoughts swept away to another time, another place. Moonlight illuminated the star-studded sky. A midnight breeze rippled through the branches of a palm tree. No longer was she Samantha, but Sabrina, alone on a lush tropical isle, alone with the man of her dreams. And he was all that she wanted... and more. Her eyes swept longingly upward to Marshall's face, lingering on the naked lines of his bronzed body. His eyes, those strange golden eyes, mirrored the hot naked desire scalding her veins. Soon... *soon* she would be carried away to a place she had never been before.

With a sigh born of envy, Samantha Monroe rested the paperback novel on slim bare thighs and gazed dreamily toward the sapphire-blue waters of the Pacific. Foam-flecked waves lapped gently on the sandy shoreline.

She could ask for little more on this beautiful June day. Today was the beginning of a well-deserved summer vacation from her teaching job at Neskowin Elementary School. It was warm and sunny, she had the beach to herself, and, as usual in her rare and precious spare time, she was totally engrossed in the latest historical romance by her favorite author.

A slim hand reached up to smooth glossy brown hair, worn in a lightly feathered style that skimmed her shoulders. What would it be like, Samantha reflected musingly in a half serious, half jesting mood, to be Sabrina, the heroine of *Love's Sweet Bondage*—to be swept off her feet by a man like Marshall, to eagerly experience all the wondrous pleasures of love....

Her eyes became reflective at the thought. She *had* been swept off her feet once, and it might indeed have been a woman's ultimate fantasy—had it lasted. Yes, she and Alan had eyes only for each other, and just as it was in her favorite romance, nothing existed save their love. But unfortunately, juggling life and love was something to which neither one of them had given any thought. She and Alan had been barely twenty, maybe too young to cope with the added pressure that love and marriage had put on their lives. She smiled rather wistfully. No, she would never again be quite so innocent or quite so blind, but it was still nice to pretend, and to hope... although it *really* was a shame that a man like Marshall Devereau existed only in a woman's imagination.

Eagerly she turned her attention to the book again.

... Marshall reached out to draw Sabrina's soft curves to his own lean hardness, his breath warm upon her cheeks as he sought her mouth with gentle hunger. She trembled against him—afraid, excited, somehow aware that no other man would ever exist for her after this night, but above all, longing desperately to learn the hidden secrets only he could teach her...

"Has the lady lost her virtue yet?"

So deeply absorbed was Samantha in envisioning the book's rapidly unfolding love scene that she nearly leaped toward the sky at the intrusive sound of the deep male voice. Unfortunately, her old and rather rickety chaise lounge took exception to the jarring motion. The next instant Samantha found herself deposited on her bottom in the sand, long legs atangle and her chair in a heap beside her.

Propping herself on one hand, she focused her startled gaze on a set of bare toes that paved the way to a pair of long muscular legs sprinkled with a fine sheen of masculine dark hairs. *And what a pair of legs they were!* She swallowed, vaguely aware of how ridiculous she must look, but conscious of a strange curling sensation in the pit of her stomach. Her eyes traveled slowly upward over a strongly muscled chest liberally covered with a mat of dark wiry curls to the man's face.

"I've had a few women fall for me—" the soft laughter in the gentle tone completely slipped by Samantha, whose eyes were huge as saucers "—but never quite so hard." When this brought no response from her, the man gave a distinctly audible sigh. "Here, let me help you up."

A hand much larger than her own effortlessly raised her from the sand, but once on her feet, Samantha still couldn't take her eyes off the man. Again her eyes roamed over the stranger's features with a look of stunned surprise.

It was Marshall Devereau, the hero of *Love's Sweet Bondage*, come to life. Except, unlike Marshall in the scene still vivid in her mind's eye, he wasn't naked—at least not quite. This man wore a pair of tight, extremely brief, dark-blue swimming trunks. He bore little resemblance to the man depicted on the paperback's suggestive cover, but he looked exactly as she, Samantha Monroe, had conjured him up in her mind—the same dark unruly brown hair, long straight nose and firmly chiseled lips.

Compelling, that's what he was, exactly the way the hero was so often described in her romance novels. And for the first time she knew *exactly* what the word meant. She caught her breath in mingled wonder and amazement.

"Hey, are you okay?"

At the glimmer of concern reflected both in his warm cocoa-brown eyes and smooth low voice, Samantha snapped out of her trance—a little.

She still couldn't take her eyes from his face. How many times had she seen those ruggedly sculpted features in her mind? Was he real? Or—heaven forbid!—an illusion? All she could manage was a shaky, "No, I—I'm fine."

"You're sure?" Warm hands skimmed the smooth bare skin of her upper arms in concerned exploration, sending a torrent of electricity vibrating through her. The man's eyes lowered to take in her skimpily clothed body. Suddenly she was acutely aware that, clad in a tiny black knit bikini, she was attired no more decently than he was.

"Yes." Her tone was breathless, but somehow she couldn't help herself. "Really, I'm fine."

"Good." He smiled, displaying a row of even white teeth, and Samantha felt as if a thousand tiny lights had exploded inside her. "Now," he said, his tone light, "since that's settled, will you tell me something?"

"S-sure." She wanted desperately to tear her eyes away from his, but there was something almost mesmerizing in those deep brown depths.

"Am *I* all right?"

Slender arched brows drew together over Samantha's deep blue eyes as she searched his face. "I think so." Her eyes were confused as they again met his. "Why do you ask?"

One corner of his mouth tipped upward in an amused smile and one dark eyebrow arched roguishly. "The way you were looking at me I was beginning to wonder if I'd suddenly sprouted a nose like

Pinocchio or a third eye in the middle of my fore-head—or maybe even both.''

An answering yet tentative smile touched Saman-tha's lips, but she dropped her lashes for a moment, realizing she was still staring. Then she answered lightly, ''No, you look—'' *perfect* was the word that came to mind, but she could hardly say that ''—fine,'' she finished hastily. This behavior was a far cry from her usual calm demeanor, and for some reason she felt compelled to explain. ''You just . . . startled me. This beach is rather secluded and I wasn't really expecting anyone.''

Even to her own ears this sounded inadequate and not entirely believable, but the man did a creditable job of hiding his reaction. He dropped his hands from her bare shoulders and his gaze sharpened for a mo-ment.

''Have we met before?''

Samantha shook her head. ''No, I'm sure we haven't.'' But a voice inside reminded her that she'd dreamed of a man like him, *exactly* like him, each and every time she picked up one of her beloved ro-mances.

Their eyes met and she felt a sudden wave of heat burn through her veins as he added softly, ''I didn't think so. I know I wouldn't have forgotten you if we had.''

He turned away and righted her chaise, then picked up her paperback from the sand, brushing a few tiny grains off the cover before handing it back to her. Sa-mantha accepted it gingerly, wondering a little at the sudden gleam in his eyes. Was he laughing at her? Rather uneasily she seated herself once again.

''You don't mind a little company, do you?''

At the sound of his voice she turned her head to find him already laying out a large beach towel on the sand, not more than a yard away from her. His shadow fell across her as she regarded him for a moment, wondering what he would say if she told him to get lost. But that was the last thing she wanted at the moment.

For two long weeks she had looked forward to this day, a day spent sunbathing and reading, reading and sunbathing, and now it seemed her well-laid plans were about to go sadly awry—though if she were honest with herself, she'd admit she didn't mind in the least. But how could she think, much less concentrate on reading, with this...this half-naked fantasy man lying beside her?

Willpower. That's what she needed. Determinedly she opened *Love's Sweet Bondage* to discover the outcome of Marshall's seduction of Sabrina. But it couldn't have been more than a few seconds before her gaze lifted and fixed on the male form stretched out beside her. The man was lying on his back, eyes closed, bristly dark lashes resting on his high cheekbones. Unable to resist, her eyes traveled slowly down his muscular chest and long well-shaped legs, returning upward to linger with breathless intensity on the place where the wiry curls on his abdomen disappeared beneath his swimsuit. He was so close that all she had to do was reach out a hand to touch the burnished skin of his shoulder, knowing instinctively that his flesh would be warm and smooth, the muscles vibrant and flowing beneath her fingertips.

Shocked by the urge to do exactly that, Samantha jerked her eyes away from the stranger and focused her attention elsewhere—to her book, since it happened to be handy. But this time the words blurred together and all she could really see was the image of the man's rugged features and tough athletic body. She blinked and swallowed, but the harder she tried to shoo away the disturbing image, the more the black print on the pages seemed to swim and float away from her.

"That must be quite a book. It seems to have you spellbound."

Spellbound. That's what she was. For once, Samantha realized it wasn't her book that held her spellbound, but a man. A man who existed not only in her mind, but in the flesh. *This* man. A deep breath and she felt her senses returning to normal.

Closing the paperback, she replaced it in the small canvas bag beside her. Looping her fingers around her knee, she smiled at the stranger rather shyly. "It is interesting," she admitted.

"Is that why you've been staring at the same word for the last five minutes?"

The question, combined with the realization that he'd been watching her all that time, sent a sudden rush of color into her cheeks. What could she say? That she was dazzled by the sun's rays glinting off the ocean? She was dazzled all right, but not by the sun.

Luckily there was no need for a response as he suddenly reached out and caught her hand in a light grasp. "I've embarrassed you, haven't I?"

"Maybe...a little." With her free hand, she pushed at a few strands of hair feathering across her cheek, returning his smile as she caught his eye. The glimmer of humor she saw there seemed to dissipate some of her natural reserve. When he smiled, which he seemed to do quite often, his face lost some of its harshness, though perhaps that wasn't quite the right description. Strong...yes, that was it. He was strong, but with a gentleness in his eyes that seemed to reach out and enfold her in its warmth.

This man was straight from the pages of a Cathryn James novel, and since Samantha was hopelessly devoted to romances, finding such a man in the flesh was almost too good to be true.

"In that case, maybe I'd better not press you for an answer to my original question." Samantha was increasingly conscious of his avid gaze roving over her features as he spoke. Did he like what he saw? She hoped so—Lord, but she hoped so!

She turned slightly to look at him. She felt silly, but she couldn't seem to stop smiling, even when he relinquished possession of her hand. "What was the question?"

"Whether or not the lady had lost her virtue yet." As her eyes widened slightly, he laughed, a low mellow sound that sent a flood of pure pleasure radiating through her body. "The lady in your book," he elaborated dryly in answer to the question in her eyes. "Definitely not you. Believe me, I wouldn't dream of being so personal. At least, not on our first meeting," he added with a twinkle in his eyes.

Will there be a second? The thought flitted through her mind, even as she laughed nervously. "Oh, that." She bit her lip and glanced over at him. "Actually, the answer is no, although I think in just a few more pages it would have been a very emphatic yes." A sudden thought struck her. "How did you know it was...well, that kind of book?"

"A steamy romance, you mean?" One corner of his mouth turned up in a lazy smile of amusement. When she nodded, he shifted his position on the towel so that he was facing her directly, his back to the gently lapping waves of the sea. "They're easy to spot," he offered in explanation. "What other book cover has a bare-chested man with his hands all over..." He stopped, his smile widening slightly as he took in Samantha's reddening cheeks. "Well, let's just say with a man touching a woman who isn't wearing a whole lot more than he is."

Samantha wasn't about to argue the point, since it was true all too often. She turned her eyes seaward for a moment, watching the white-crested silvery waves against the blue horizon. Several children scampered through the rolling surf, their cries of laughter echoing through the air. Her eyes drifted back to the stranger. "Do you do much reading yourself?" she asked curiously.

There was a slight twitch to the man's lips as if he was trying very hard to hold back a grin, but Samantha was much more involved in watching the play of muscles in his bare shoulders as he shrugged to really notice. "I've been known to frequent a few bookstores."

"Do you live around here?" There, it was out, the question she'd been wanting to ask since she'd first seen him. She held her breath, waiting almost painfully for his answer. Neskowin was a small town on the central Oregon coast; most tourists thronged to the larger towns north or south of the community, although a number of vacation homes nestled along this stretch of beach. Her own small house was bordered by one, though she'd never met the owner.

"No. I'm vacationing, although I expect to get a lot of work done while I'm here," he said with a lift of both dark brows.

How long was he staying? A week? Two weeks? And *where* was he staying? Was he married? No, somehow she knew he wasn't, and besides, her subconscious mind had already noted the absence of a wedding ring. She'd have liked to give voice to the questions tumbling around in her head, but somehow the words couldn't find their way out past the knot in her throat. Instead she murmured, "I see."

"How about you? Are you vacationing, too?"

Samantha smiled, pleased at his interest. "No, I live here." She gestured over her shoulder toward a small whitewashed house surrounded by a cluster of gnarled windblown trees just beyond the beach. "That's my house back there."

He looked over her shoulder, his eyebrows lifting in surprise. "You live here year-round? I thought most of the homes here were summer places."

"Mine is one of the few that isn't. It's very quiet and peaceful—" she smiled, her gaze resting on her book for a fleeting second "—and although the town isn't booming with nightlife, I like it here."

"What's your name?"

"Samantha," she told him. "Samantha Monroe." She leaned forward and rested her arms on her knees. The sun beat down on her back, but the shimmering warmth felt good on her bare skin. She was just about to ask a few questions of her own when his eyes caught hers and she found herself admiring him again.

"So tell me, Samantha," he said easily, his eyes never leaving hers, "what do you do in this life besides sunbathe on the beach on lazy June afternoons? Are you a—" he smiled as if he already knew the answer "—a member of the idle rich?"

Samantha laughed, a low tinkling sound that floated away on the brisk sea breeze. "Not exactly. I teach second grade at the elementary school here, and since school is out for the summer," she stated the obvious, "that explains why I'm idle—at the moment. And as for being rich, my savings account is practically down to zilch since I've been putting every spare nickel and dime I earn into fixing up my house. It wasn't exactly in mint condition when I bought it, but it's beginning to shape up pretty well."

"Mmm," he agreed, though from the direction his eyes were looking, it wasn't the shape of her house he was assessing, but rather the shape of her long slender legs. She felt a momentary discomfort and resisted the impulse to tug at the bottom of her bikini briefs to hide the back of her thighs. But when his eyes rested once again on her face, she knew an undeniable but all too brief thrill of satisfaction at the flare of undisguised appreciation in his eyes.

He tipped his head to the side and studied her for a moment. "So you're a schoolteacher," he murmured. "It fits...to a degree."

She stretched out her legs in a smooth supple motion and leaned back again. "To a degree?" she repeated, a little surprised at how much at ease she was with this stranger, despite the rather delirious way she felt when she looked at him.

He nodded and gave her a lopsided grin. "On one hand, you hardly seem like the typical schoolmarm of old—prim and proper, stern and straitlaced—the type who won't stand any nonsense and who reigns over her classroom with a ruler in one hand and a paddle in the other."

"Sounds like my eighth-grade teacher, Mrs. Webster," Samantha recalled. "She was about six feet tall with iron-gray hair that she wore in a tightly coiled bun, and I never saw her smile *once* that entire year." She laughed. "I can't say I've ever had much of a discipline problem with my second-graders, though I'll admit you're right. I certainly wouldn't look to a paddle as the solution.''

"I think I know *why* you've never had any problem. All the little boys in your class probably had a crush on you, and all the little girls undoubtedly wanted to grow up to be just like you.''

"I'm not so sure about that," Samantha said with a grin, "but I do know that if I ever see another shiny red apple again in my lifetime, it'll be too soon. And to think I believed that was a thing of the past!''

His laughter joined hers for a moment before he spoke again. "You do give the impression of being rather quiet and studious, though, so I can't say I'm surprised to find your head buried in a book." He watched her for a few seconds, an easy smile lifting the corners of his firm mouth. "But I *am* surprised by your choice of... reading material.''

Samantha tilted her head and regarded him inquisitively. "Why?''

"A teacher who likes romances?" There was a gleam of laughter in his eyes as he shaded them from the bright glare of the sun. "What would your students say if they knew you were reading tales of lust and passion? Worse yet, what would their parents think?''

She could hardly take offense at his jesting tone. "They would probably think I was disgracefully depraved," she said primly, then added with a grin, "or exceedingly deprived." She flipped her hair over her shoulder and smiled at him. "But just to reassure you, I'll have you know I have a healthy appreciation for Steinbeck and Hemingway and I've read every single word of *War and Peace!*''

His eyes were a warm shade of toasty brown as he gazed across at her. "I think," he said dryly, "I've just discovered the true meaning of the phrase 'properly chastised.'"

A tingle of excitement raced down her spine at his look. She attempted to cover it by observing flippantly, "And you seem to be rather well versed in historical romance jargon for a man."

The stranger's smile deepened. "What would you say if I told you I'd read a few?"

It took a moment for his words to sink in, but when they did, Samantha's eyes widened. She observed his relaxed position on the sand, his bronzed skin a sharp contrast to the fluffy white beach towel. He looked very virile and totally masculine sitting there so casually, and yet...something told her he was perfectly serious.

A man who read romances—*women's* romances. With an effort she forced her eyes to meet his. "How...unusual."

"Yes, I suppose it is." A cocky grin split his lean features. "But just for the record, I only did it out of curiosity—and duty."

Duty? This was growing stranger by the moment, she thought to herself. She was on the verge of questioning him further when he reached out a long arm and plucked her paperback from the bag between them. "As a matter of fact—" there was a smile in his voice as he stared at the cover "—I'm rather familiar with this author's books."

"You are?" A strange feeling of pleasure surged through her as she slipped her legs over the side of her chair and wiggled her toes in the warm sand. "What a coincidence," she said, eyes sparkling with sudden enthusiasm. "Cathryn James is my favorite author. I love the way she writes and I never miss *any* of her books."

"Hmm," was his only comment. He rose lithely to his feet and took a single step backward. Her eyes followed his form, and she suddenly realized he was leaving. Of all the luck, she thought to herself irritably. The dream of a lifetime and he was walking out the door after barely sticking his foot inside. What a lousy way to start a vacation!

But someone upstairs must have been watching out for her. She could hardly believe it when he held out a hand to her. "How about a walk on the beach with me?"

"Sure." It was all she could do to restrain herself from doing handsprings on the sand—as if she knew how—but she let him pull her up beside him.

"Tell me something," he said, looking down at her. "How do you say the name of this place?"

"Neskowin?" When he nodded, she smiled. "Neskow-in. Slight accent on the first syllable, silent *w*." The dazzling smile he gave her nearly took her breath away, but they hadn't gone more than a few steps when she tugged on his hand and halted. She glanced up at him, her look playful, as a belated thought suddenly occurred to her. "It might be nice if I knew who I was walking on the beach with."

His lips turned up in a barely discernible smile as he looked down into her upturned face. "Jason," he supplied softly.

"Jason...?" To her surprise, at her question, he stopped and bowed down low before her with a flourish. When he returned to an upright position, his smile was transformed into a full-blown grin.

"Jason Armstrong is my name—" there was a brief but very effective pause "—also known as Cathryn James."

Two

___

Samantha stared at him for a moment, almost—just almost—tempted to believe he was actually serious. Then she turned on her heel and ambled down the beach, tossing back a comment over her shoulder.

"Sure you are. And I'm Norman Mailer."

Jason Armstrong caught up with her easily, his long-legged form falling in beside her. "You don't believe me?"

She sent him a sidelong glance. "Mr. Armstrong—"

"Jason. Call me Jason."

"All right then." She gave him a saccharine smile and said mildly, "Not that I'm trying to criticize, but you are sadly in need of a lesson with regard to the written word—"

"Aha, now you're beginning to sound like the teacher you are."

She lifted a slender brow in reproach and continued, "Men write science-fiction stories, fantasy and adventure stories—"

"Sleazy adventure stories?"

"Well, yes—" she frowned slightly at him "—with a lot of sex and violence—"

"And your romances aren't full of sex?"

"Not in the way you're thinking," she reproved confidently. "They're love stories, and there's a world of difference between love and sex." She halted, planting her feet firmly in the soft sand to look up at him. "Even if you are a writer—which I'm not sure you are—you certainly couldn't write a romance."

"You sound very sure of yourself." He smiled down at her, laughter flickering in his eyes.

"I am. I've read dozens of romances, both historical and contemporary, but I've *never* read one written by a man—"

"Oh, yes, you have." His tone was very soft, almost caressing.

Samantha glowered up at him, beginning to wonder why he was persisting in his little joke. "I haven't," she insisted, a bit more bitingly than she intended. Taking a deep breath, she ran her fingers upward through the soft hair lying on her nape. "Look, I don't know why you insist on—"

"Would you rather have me lie?"

"No, of course not." The tiniest bit of exasperation was beginning to gnaw at her, but as his eyes held hers, she saw something in the chocolaty-brown depths that caused a niggle of doubt to enter her brain. He couldn't possibly be serious... or could he?

She let him lead her over to a huge chunk of whitewashed driftwood near the edge of the sand. With a gentle hand on her shoulder he pushed her down to a sitting position.

"This is just beginning to get interesting," he said as he sat down beside her.

Samantha eyed him rather warily. "What is?"

"Your views on why a man couldn't possibly write a romance." His eyes were full of mirth and his mouth kept twitching as if he was barely able to contain his laughter.

Again Samantha experienced a tiny spurt of doubt. She gazed at him hesitantly. "You really are a writer?"

"I really am a writer," he assured her. "And I make a very good living at it."

"A fiction writer?"

"A fiction writer. Now if you don't mind, pray tell me why you think a man couldn't possibly write one of your precious romances."

Samantha breathed a sigh of relief. At least this time he wasn't insisting he was Cathryn James! "Well—" a thoughtful frown creased her forehead for a moment "—for one thing, I just can't see a man being able to get into the head of a woman the way another woman could."

"Cathryn James writes from a dual point of view, if you recall. The hero's thoughts and feelings are just as much in evidence as the heroine's."

Samantha's eyes flickered away from his steady gaze and she shifted uneasily. "Yes, that's true, but…" She stopped, not sure she wanted to go ahead with what she'd been about to say.

"But what?"

Jason lifted one of her hands from her thigh and began to lightly trace a pattern in the palm of her hand.

Her breath caught in her throat. His touch sent a wild swirl of emotion rushing through her. She was suddenly, acutely aware of the hairy thigh pressed against the smoothness of her own. Her heart fluttered wildly in her breast.

"The emotional intensity," she began uncertainly, "particularly in the love scenes—" she swallowed, her voice a mere thread of sound, low and very hushed "—and especially Cathryn James's books, is described in such a way that...that when I read those scenes, it's as if I'm actually there." She paused for a fleeting second to sum up her rather tumultuous thoughts. "It's the emotion that touches me, knowing what the heroine is feeling and..."

"Go on," he urged softly when she hesitated. His fingers feathered up to stroke the soft skin on the inside of her wrist and Samantha had to consciously will her mind away from the feeling of excitement he roused in her.

"And no man could possibly describe how a woman feels inside, what she's thinking, when a man is...making love to her." Was she actually sitting here discussing sex with a man she'd just met?

"But what about men?" His low voice broke into her thoughts. "Are we incapable of the same emotions, are we heartless and unresponsive? Do you think that we don't feel the same way a woman does when a man touches her?" A finger under her chin gently turned her face to his, and she stared upward into Jason's rugged features, mesmerized by the liquid heat glowing in his eyes. "And she touches him?"

"I—I don't know." What a question, and for him to ask it now—now when she felt as if she was being turned inside out, her body vaporizing into a vast sea of sensations as his hands cupped her bare shoulders and his palms glided smoothly down her arms.

"A little insight and a little imagination is all it takes." Jason's murmured words were low and husky, his breath warm and caressing as it fanned her cheeks. "Do you want me to tell you how you feel, Samantha?"

"I...no, no!" Her heart beat furiously in her chest. She was trapped in a haze of conflicting emotions. She wanted to pull away, *knew* she should pull away, but her limbs felt curiously heavy and lethargic, while inside she was strangely agitated, wanting, wondering, hoping this wouldn't end before it had even started.

Jason's hands moved up to frame her face, the pads of his thumbs tracing the delicate contours of her cheekbones over and over again before finding the throbbing pulse beneath her jawline. "You like this, don't you?" he asked softly. Samantha nodded, unable to find the strength to speak, or to deny the involuntary response of her body. "Your heart is pounding like a drum, your breath is coming as fast as if you've just run a four-minute mile...." His lips parted to reveal the strong even whiteness of his teeth. "This is exciting to you, isn't it?"

Somehow she managed to shake her head this time. "No...stop!"

"Not yet." He moved his dark head closer, the words whispered against her cheek, stirring the soft tendrils of hair near her ear. "It's your turn, Samantha. As the saying goes, turnabout is fair play."

Her hands were lifted and placed against his shoulders. Confused, she raised her gaze to his, unprepared for the compelling glitter in his eyes—yet it thrilled her clear to the tips of her toes. "Go ahead," he chided softly, his voice curiously unsteady. "Touch me. Feel me. Do—anything you want."

The feel of the firm bronzed flesh beneath her fingertips and the chance to explore the sleek skin of his nearly naked body as she had so longed to do earlier, were too potent a temptation to deny. Her breath quickened even more in anticipation as her hands glided over the sinewy muscles of his arms in silent reciprocation of his actions. She heard his harsh intake of breath at her first tentative touch and lifted her eyes again. A curious sense of power filled her as she beheld the fierce glow in his eyes once more.

Emboldened by his unexpected response, Samantha slid her slim tapered fingers up the strong column of his neck, delighting in the slightly roughened texture of his clean-shaven jawline. Her other hand rested lightly on the broad landscape of his chest, fingers twined seductively in the silky dark jungle of curly hair. As her fingers moved to explore the hard contours of his mouth, she could feel the slow steady beat of his heart increase its rhythm beneath her hand.

It was unthinkable that she should be behaving this way with a man she barely knew—so totally out of character for her. But nothing really seemed to matter. She closed her eyes, reveling in this strange sensation, her senses expanding, widening, reaching out to absorb the heat that seemed to flow from her body into Jason's, his into hers . . .

"You see?" His throaty whisper broke into the hazy shroud of pleasure surrounding her. "Would it be so hard for a person to describe the way you feel—what both of us feel?"

Samantha drew back a little, reluctant to break away from him, not wanting to shatter the web of enchantment he had spun so easily around her. Jason

Armstrong was magic. There was magic in his voice, magic in his touch, magic in his words.

"Not for a writer." A soft smile curved her mouth, and this time the inflection of disbelief was gone from her tone. "Are you really Cathryn James?"

"In the flesh," he said softly, tipping her face up to his to search her eyes. "Are you disappointed?"

"No," she answered honestly. Thunderstruck, maybe, but not disappointed, she thought to herself. But a second later a thought suddenly pricked her. She bit her lip and added quietly, "But I'm not sure you needed to go to such lengths to prove your point."

"The end justifies the means, you see," Jason said with a shrug that might have been an apology. "And while the motive and method might have been on Cathryn's behalf—" he studied her openly, his look growing more and more intent "—this is for me."

Before she could divine his meaning, his head blotted out the shimmering glare of the sun and her mouth was claimed with an urgency that left her breathless. Her hands caught at his shoulders, fingers clutching at the taut flesh as waves of pleasure swept through her, stronger than anything she'd ever thought possible. Jason's arms drew her closer, his fingers tightening almost convulsively on the soft flesh of her hips for just a moment.

"Miss Monroe! Hey, Miss Monroe!"

Recovering her senses far more quickly than she'd have expected under the circumstances, Samantha drew back from the circle of Jason's arms in time to see a small figure racing toward her.

"Hello, Kevin." Samantha couldn't help but smile at the towheaded youngster sporting a broad toothless grin who halted before her in a spray of sand.

"Notice anything different about me, Miss Monroe?"

Samantha reached out and gently pinched his sunburned cheek. "You lost your other front tooth. Did you pull it out yourself, champ?"

"Nope," the little boy proudly announced. "It fell out while I was eating an apple just a few minutes ago and there was blood all over..." Samantha stifled a groan, glad when Kevin decided to go no further. He was hopping from one foot to the other, barely able to control his excitement. "Hey, you want me to go get one for you? My mom brought a whole bunch along with us."

She exchanged a subtle look of amusement with Jason, who was looking on quietly. "No, thanks, Kevin." She bit her lip, trying hard not to laugh as she saw a slight tremor at Jason's mouth, as well. "I, um, I just had lunch not long ago and I'm really not very hungry."

Kevin's vivid blue eyes lost their hopeful gleam. "You sure?"

"I'm sure," she said gently. Then, at his crestfallen expression, she added, "Maybe next time. You will come and see me again, won't you?"

The little boy's face brightened immediately. "You betcha! I sure do miss you, Miss Monroe, even though I just saw you a couple days ago."

"I miss you, too, Kevin." Samantha reached out and ruffled his blond curls.

"I guess I better get back to my mom now. She told me not to bother you for long." He grinned up at her, then sent a shy but curious glance at Jason. "See ya later, Miss Monroe. Bye, Mr. Monroe."

Samantha laughed aloud as Jason's thick eyebrows shot up at Kevin's departing address. "Mr. Monroe?'' he echoed doubtfully, amusement flickering in the eyes that met hers. ''I think I've just been adopted—'' his gaze grew warmer by degrees as it continued to rest on her flushed cheeks ''—but you know, I think I like the idea.''

She couldn't help but respond to his bantering tone. ''But if you misbehave, I'll have to send you home to—'' She stopped and looked at him quizzically.

''Los Angeles.'' His devastating smile sent waves of heat pouring through her veins. ''I don't think you have to worry about it, though. I'll be close enough that you can keep an eye on me practically every minute of the day.''

And night? Unbidden, the words came tumbling into her mind. The thought, as well as the memory of his recent kiss, kindled a kind of restless longing in her body. She turned her eyes away from his hurriedly, watching distractedly as the frothy surf raced toward them. But curiosity and maybe even reckless hope made her ask, ''And just how close would that be?''

''Right next door.''

Surprise widened her eyes before a hint of disbelief came into them. ''That house is owned by a man named David Winters who lives in Portland, not Los Angeles,'' she said evenly, wondering if she'd been duped after all. ''And he isn't a writer, he's—''

''An advertising executive,'' Jason finished for her smugly, and quite correctly.

Samantha frowned good-naturedly. ''Next I suppose you're going to tell me that besides having a triple identity, you lead some kind of a double life.''

''Nothing quite so melodramatic,'' he said with a chuckle. ''David is an old college buddy of mine. He's letting me use his place for the summer.'' A long finger reached out to tilt her chin up to his. "So tell me. Do you mind having me as a neighbor all summer?"

Samantha's heart fluttered wildly at his words. The whole summer—he was staying the whole summer! Part of her wanted to stand up and shout for joy while another part was very much afraid the word "neighbor"—people who nodded a civil hello on the way to the car or smiled politely while picking up the mail— would dictate the bounds of their relationship.

She forced a light tone. "Of course not. So long as you don't peck away at your typewriter all night long or come pounding on my door at six in the morning to borrow the newspaper. I'm an absolute bear if I don't get my eight hours beauty sleep."

"I won't bother knocking then." With his even noncommittal tone it was hard to tell if he was serious, but a quick glance revealed a tiny network of fine lines extending outward from his eyes, visible only when he smiled. "And as for getting your beauty sleep," he added, "you've obviously been getting plenty."

Samantha looked away in confusion. She supposed she was attractive enough, but she would never have called herself pretty. Her mouth was a little too wide, her nose too pert and uptilted, her hair a mousy brown. Of average height, her body was supple but lean. In high school she'd often despaired of having any bustline at all. "You're just a late bloomer," her mother had often laughed. And her mother had been right, though Samantha had thought the time would never come. But even now that her breasts were nicely rounded, her hips slightly fuller, she considered her eyes her best asset. Large and widely spaced, they were a clear shade of blue, which was further enhanced by a thick fringe of lashes.

Pushing herself off the chunk of driftwood with both hands, she got to her feet. She ignored the warm rush of color staining her cheeks at Jason's knowing glance, once again conscious of the brevity of both their suits.

"Shall we get back?" she said quickly. "My house is unlocked and I don't like to stay away for long."

Jason glanced at his watch, a look of obvious reluctance on his face as he rose to his feet. "I suppose so. I have a long drive ahead of me yet this afternoon."

"So soon?" she asked curiously. "You just said you were staying for the summer."

"Oh, I am. But I'm being interviewed on a radio talk show tonight in Seattle."

"Coming out of the closet?" Samantha asked, unable to hold back a smile.

"In a way." He shrugged. "Word leaked out about a year ago that I was the man behind Cathryn James. My publisher wasn't exactly overjoyed until they found out it actually seemed to boost sales."

"Why did they mind so much?"

"It was my publisher's recommendation that I write under a female pseudonym," he explained. "They didn't think women would buy a romance written by a man." He looked at her out of the corner of his eye and raised a mocking eyebrow. "Sound familiar?"

"Now I'm the one who's been 'properly chastised,'" Samantha responded dryly. They lapsed into a companionable silence as they picked their way through a smattering of broken seashells and around a clump of seaweed, their bare feet weaving a meandering trail behind them in the sun-warmed sand.

When they neared her small sequestered home, Samantha's steps faltered. She was admittedly reluctant to see him leave so soon. Taking a deep breath, she turned to him. "Would you like to come in for a drink? That is, if you have time."

A quick glance at his watch and Jason assured her with a decided gleam in his eyes, "Just enough time. Lead the way, fair lady."

As she entered through the back screen door, golden rays of sunlight streamed through maple-stained shutters, which she had left ajar in her compact kitchen. Jason followed her. Her bare feet padded silently across the spotless tiled floor toward the refrigerator. After a hasty glance inside, she bit her lip and turned toward him. "I hope you don't mind orange juice or iced tea. I don't usually keep liquor on hand unless I'm expecting company."

"Iced tea will be fine," he said easily. "I don't drink much anyway, especially with a lady around." Samantha sent him a quizzical glance over her shoulder as she reached for the pitcher of iced tea. "It befuddles the mind," he explained, an almost wicked glint in his eyes, "and dulls the senses."

"Not to mention what it does to a man's ability," she muttered under her breath, knowing full well she had fallen right into his trap. She poured the tea into two large chilled glasses and handed one to him.

"That goes without saying." He took a long draft of the amber-colored liquid, then grinned at her. "Can't say I've ever had that problem, though."

Looking at his trim muscular form, she could see why. The man positively reeked of virility, to say nothing of the very potent attraction he would possess for many a woman. But for some reason, his response irked her to no end.

"Well," she muttered, turning on her heel and walking into the living room, "I don't suppose you could write the kind of love scenes you do without at least *some* experience."

"I suppose," Jason agreed mildly. He sat down across from her as she curled up on her favorite velour chair. His mouth twitched with amusement as he took in her suddenly distant expression. "Would you like it better if I didn't include sex scenes in my books? Your face looks like it might splinter into a thousand pieces if you even attempted a smile."

When she refused to say anything, he pressed further. "I write it and you read it," he said with a shrug. "So which of us would you call the worst degenerate?"

"I don't think either one of us is," she admitted grudgingly after a moment's silence. It wasn't the inclusion of sex in his novels that bothered her. Heaven knew she felt like melting into a mass of sizzling nerve endings when she read his love scenes. It was the fact that he might be drawing on his own experiences while writing them. She knew she had no right to feel this way, but the thought was little comfort.

"I think the difference between us lies in what you just said," she added with a slight bite to her tone. "You call them sex scenes and I think of them as love scenes."

Jason studied her averted profile silently, his smile slowly fading. "I guess that's what they're intended to be," he finally murmured.

Samantha blinked, then frowned. "Don't you know?" she demanded. "You certainly should— you've written dozens of love scenes! Why, love is what makes these books so special! Sex is nothing more than a biological function, a chemical reaction! I've read enough romances to know the difference between an author who writes sex scenes and an author who writes love scenes, and yours are definitely love scenes!''

''I write what the reader expects and what my publisher wants. In my opinion, my sex scenes—or rather *love* scenes—are a bit idealistic.'' He swirled the ice in his glass and shrugged indifferently. ''Making love is physically fulfilling, emotionally satisfying, but as far as inducing a blissful state of euphoria *a la* the romance novel—'' he gave her a half-smile ''—let's face it. These books are little more than fantasy.''

Samantha stared at him incredulously, her momentary ire all but forgotten. ''Just what are we talking about here—love or making love?''

Jason smiled blandly. ''I have the feeling you equate the two.''

''Forgive me for being such a daydreamer—'' her tone was even, but she could hardly believe what she was hearing ''—but yes, that's how I see it. Love is more than just a state of mind, and making love should be the ultimate expression of the way two people feel about each other. Without it, it doesn't mean a thing!'' And that was how it had been for her and Alan, at least at first, especially at first. They had been wildly, madly in love their first year together, but two more years of marriage had found them drifting apart. And she knew from experience that once the feelings began to wane, so did the magic.

When Jason merely smiled and shrugged his shoulders dismissively, she leaned forward, her hands curling into fists on her thighs. ''In *Conquer the Wind*, your heroine said that the way she felt was like—'' she searched for the phrase, snapping her fingers when she remembered ''—heaven on earth. Are you saying that was pure bunk?''

"Oh, yes, the fair Rosalind," he murmured, crossing his long legs at the knee as if he hadn't a care in the world. "You, like Rosalind, have been bitten by the happily-ever-after bug. And maybe it's not pure bunk, but it's certainly exaggerated."

Samantha's temper was off and running at his casual manner and offhand words. "What about this afternoon at the beach?" she charged hotly, cold fury beginning to burn inside her. This was deceit of the worst kind! "That bit about men feeling the same way women do—what was that? Exploitation? Research for your next book? When you said it was for *Cathryn's* benefit you certainly weren't kidding! The high and mighty Jason Armstrong certainly wouldn't have spoken so humbly! He's too much of a cynic, isn't he? I'll give you one thing, though, you're an even better writer than I thought for being able to fabricate that kind of emotional intensity!"

She felt a brief moment of triumph at the startled look on his face, the momentary confusion in his eyes as if she'd pointed out something he hadn't really considered. But when his features relaxed into that now-familiar but oh-so-maddening smile, it was too much. Samantha jumped up and started to brush past him, only to find herself caught around the waist and dragged down beside him on the couch.

"What's the rush?" he murmured into her ear.

As her bare skin pressed against the naked warmth of his furry chest, her pulses skittered alarmingly, but she ignored the sudden racing of her heart. "You're on your way to Seattle, remember?" she pointed out furiously. "I'm merely obliging you by leaving so you can be on your merry way!" This time when she started to rise, both of Jason's arms snaked around her and he held her firmly in place, grinning down into her mutinous face.

"Isn't this where you say, 'Let me go, you beast!'?"

Samantha didn't even bat an eyelash at his hysterical falsetto. She glared up at him, holding herself rigidly away from him, which proved to be nearly a circus feat due to his constricting grip. The dratted man was barely giving her room to breathe!

"A show of brute strength might be expected in one of your novels, Jason Armstrong," she announced tautly, "but as you so aptly pointed out, romances are pure fantasy, and I'm not about to reenact a scene from one of *your* books—or anyone else's."

"Why not? You might enjoy... a small dalliance." There was a gleam in his eye as he added hopefully, "Or maybe a big one?"

Samantha stared at the smooth firmness of the mouth smiling ever so slightly above hers. She suppressed an inward tremor and wished her earlier indignation would return to swamp the sudden churning of her insides. If only his breath on her cheeks was not so warm, so inviting.

"I don't think so," she said in a voice that wasn't entirely steady. "You see, I expect fireworks and sky-rockets, and maybe even a few shooting stars, and you've already told me I won't get that." She took a deep breath, finally finding the strength to turn her head aside. "And frankly, I'd be disappointed with anything less."

She could see that she had surprised him again, but this time felt no elation as she had before. The mocking light faded from his eyes but his smile was still faintly teasing as he looked down at her.

"To think I was actually looking forward to subduing a feisty wench just like one of my heroes," he said lightly. His arms dropped from her body. "And instead I find my head on the chopping block." He stared down at her motionless form, his eyes almost somber as they swept over her body. "We're bound to run into each other again this summer. Maybe we'll see each other soon."

"Maybe," she echoed quietly, watching uneasily as his long legs carried him across the floor and out the front door.

It seemed that, like it or not, she was stuck with Jason Armstrong for the summer, and right now the idea wasn't quite as appealing as it had been earlier.

Samantha did a fairly creditable job of dismissing Jason from her mind that day. But when she crawled into bed that night, she found herself reliving his kiss on the beach, the feel of his hands on her body.

Sighing defeatedly, she switched on the bedside lamp and reached for the copy of *Love's Sweet Bondage*. But as she stared at the cover, a curious thing happened. The idea of reading Cathryn James's—or rather Jason Armstrong's—romantic storytelling suddenly lost all its appeal for her.

Almost as if she was saying farewell to an old friend she would never see again, she dropped the book in the wicker wastebasket near her bedside, conscious of an almost painful ache of her breast.

The memory of Jason's touch still filled her with a sense of wonder and excitement, perhaps even awe, but the magic of his words had palled . . . for the moment.

And maybe even for good.

Three

Golden sunlight streaming through pristine white curtains prodded Samantha into wakefulness the next morning. With a muffled groan, she rolled onto her back and threw an arm over her eyes. Her lids drifted peacefully closed and she was ready to doze off again when suddenly a curious feeling prickled her skin.

Her eyes flew open as she quickly sat up, muscles tensed and ready to spring from the bed. "You!" she gasped at the sight of Jason Armstrong sitting nonchalantly on the side of her bed. "What are you doing in here?"

His grin was all too disarming, that beautifully shaped mouth was doing strange things to her insides. Samantha swiftly fought down the alarming flutter of her pulse. "I couldn't find you anywhere else," he said cheerfully.

"But you—you're in my bedroom! And—you're supposed to be in Seattle." Eyes that had been wide with shock narrowed suddenly. "Why didn't you ring the doorbell? Or at least knock?"

"I was in Seattle," he said mildly. "I missed you, so I drove back last night and got in early this morning. And as for knocking...well, I told you yesterday I wouldn't bother." There was a sudden twinkle in his deep brown eyes. "Serves you right, though, for leaving your door unlocked again. You're lucky it was me and not some other—" his look sharpened as his eyes ran boldly down her body, the gauzy material of her nightie concealing precious little of her flesh "—degenerate," he finally finished, his eyes lingering on the gentle thrust of her breasts.

Samantha grabbed wildly for the sheet. The fact that she'd forgotten to lock her door last night took a back seat to the wholly masculine glint of appreciation in his eyes. When Jason leaned toward her, she flung out her other hand, her palm slapping against the unyielding muscle of his shoulder as she attempted to thwart his forward motion.

"Don't!" she gasped, her eyes running over his wide shoulders and naked hair-roughened flesh. Like the previous day, he wore only a brief pair of shorts. "My God, I know for a fact you're not a struggling writer scrimping and scraping for a living anymore! What have you got against buying clothes—and wearing them!"

"Writers and artists are well-known for their eccentricities. And besides, I just finished a three-mile jog on the beach," he murmured, his mouth a mere breath away from hers. "And I came to see if what you said was true."

Even as he spoke, Samantha could feel a slight film of moisture beneath her fingertips where they curled around his shoulder. A languorous feeling pervaded her limbs, but she resisted the urge to explore the length of his back and the sinewy strength of his biceps, tautly defined as he rested both hands against the mattress.

She swallowed nervously, stringently avoiding eye contact with him, as if that would somehow make her less aware of his overpowering maleness. "If what was true?"

"That you're a bear in the morning—like you said you were."

"I was right, wasn't I?" Her voice was little more than a ribbon of sound, her heart was beginning to thump with heavy, uneven strokes against her ribs. She really should be telling him to get off her bed and out of her house, maybe even out of her life. And she would—eventually.

"Maybe." He smiled and added lazily, "And then again, maybe not."

The soft velvet of his voice was as potent as a caress. His eyes rested on her parted lips. Samantha's head tilted back in unconscious invitation as he leaned closer still, the delicate arch of her neck drawing his attention away from her mouth. She felt the extremely heady sensation of his lips slowly journeying upward against the sensitive cord on the side of her neck.

A soft sigh escaped her when his mouth closed over hers. His arms enfolded her, gathering her body close to the solid warmth of his chest. She felt strangely giddy, light-headed, totally unlike herself. But then, ever since this man had first stepped into her life yesterday, she hadn't been feeling quite like herself. She

led a placid, extremely tranquil existence. Only one
other time had she acted so irrationally—and look
where it had led. Disastrous was a harsh word to describe her marriage, but certainly it had been a disappointment. After all, she'd thought it would last
forever.

No, it wasn't often she was given to impulse; it
wasn't often she let her emotions carry her away so
quickly. But all thought of that long-ago time with
Alan and anything else were quickly banished from
her mind, and all she could think of was this man who
seemed able to charm her at will. She was awash in a
sea of sensation, acutely and vibrantly aware of
everything about Jason—the smooth feel of his muscles beneath her fingers, the warm compelling touch
of his mouth moving so enticingly on hers and the
heady feeling it aroused, as well as the queer feeling
that shot through her and made her fairly ache to explore every taut inch of his spare muscular body.

"Mmm, that was nice," Jason whispered into her
hair when he finally lifted his head from hers a long
time later. Samantha was left with a burning desire for
another kiss—and more.

"Better than nice—it was fantastic."

She opened her eyes as she realized the husky voice
had come from her own throat. Had she actually said
that? She tried not to look stricken, but when Jason
laughed softly she found her lips curving in an answering smile. She gasped with delight when his lips
found the smooth skin of her shoulder once more before he slid away from her.

As he stood up, he glanced idly at the nightstand.
Samantha held her breath as his eyes sharpened, low-
ering to the small wastebasket below it. Bending over,

he retrieved the copy of *Love's Sweet Bondage* she had thrown out the night before.

A slight frown was etched between his dark eyebrows as Samantha met his eyes uneasily. "I've never known a faithful fan who threw away her favorite author's books. At the very least, you could have given it to someone else. Didn't you like the ending?"

Damn, of all the things for him to notice! "I'm sure I would have liked it—" she smoothed a fold of the blanket and looked away "—had I gotten that far."

Jason moved a step closer, his shadow falling across her and somehow making the moment seem almost ominous. "How far did you get?"

"Only—as far as I got yesterday on the beach," she said in a low voice, feeling unaccountably guilty. "Less than halfway through."

"I thought you liked it."

"I . . . I did."

"Then why throw it out before you even finished it?"

Samantha shook her head, not quite sure how to respond. "I'm not sure you want to know," she said finally.

"Oh, yes, I do." Again Jason sat down on the bed. His mouth was smiling, but his eyes seemed to hold a challenge. "My biggest fan turned critic—this could be very enlightening."

Samantha's mouth tightened at the sarcastic drawl. Before she had felt like cringing inside, now sensing his displeasure, she was determined to give him no quarter. "All right then," she said, drawing a deep breath and looking him straight in the eye. "I couldn't read it because after finding out what you're really like, I'd have felt cheated. Maybe it's *idealistic* of me—" she emphasized the word with a downward curl of her lips ''—but I like to think an author believes in what he's writing about. And frankly, reading one of your books now would be almost...'' She halted, groping for the right word, her eyes flashing triumphantly when she found it. ''Almost sacrilegious.''

Jason blinked in surprise, and his thick eyebrows drew together over that long straight nose before he smiled thinly. ''So you don't like my philosophy on love. Is that what this is about?''

''Yes.'' She folded her arms firmly over the sheet where it covered her breasts and fixed defiant eyes on him. Now that she'd made her stand, she wasn't about to back down.

''And as for my books, you'd like me to say I write about love for the sake of love—because of my unswerving faith and belief in it.''

She hesitated. She would like to hear that, but not if it wasn't true, and right now, if he swore on a stack of Bibles, she knew she'd never be able to believe him.

''It's too bad I broke your bubble, but believe it or not, I do write for love—love of money.'' There was a brief pause. ''Although I suppose it's never too late to change.''

Was that a twinge of regret she saw in his eyes? It was gone before she could really be sure. ''Oh, don't worry,'' she said brazenly. ''You know the saying about one bad apple? Well, just because I won't be reading any more of your books doesn't mean I've read my last romance. There are plenty of good authors out there and I'm sure I'll find a replacement in no time!''

He merely smiled at this as if she'd said something immensely amusing. ''Are you a good teacher?'' he inquired blandly.

The abrupt change in subject caught her by surprise. She glanced at him quickly. "I've only taught for two years," she said slowly, "but I didn't have any complaints and I was satisfied with my students' progress." She eyed him rather warily. "Yes, I'd say I'm a good teacher."

"Good." He nodded, a decidedly wicked gleam in his eyes. "So give me an education—a lesson to last a lifetime. Show me how wrong I am about . . . love."

Samantha stared at him for what must have been a full minute. Talk about unpredictable, she thought to herself disbelievingly. Jason Armstrong was certainly that! She resisted the impulse to pull away from him when he reached out a forefinger and began to stroke the soft skin stretched across her collarbone.

"Jason Armstrong," she began carefully, "I wouldn't touch that offer with an insulated ten-foot pole." Come to think of it, about ten feet of insulation was exactly what she needed. Maybe then she wouldn't feel so shivery both inside and out the minute he touched her.

"Where's your sense of adventure?" That teasing voice contained more than a measure of cajolery. "Don't you ever crave a little excitement?"

"No," she retorted tartly. "My sense of adventure and excitement doesn't extend beyond occasionally trying a bargain-brand product at the grocery store."

"Oh, come on. The way I see it neither one of us can come out the loser."

Samantha drew a deep breath. Was it his male ego talking again? He certainly seemed to have been blessed with a healthy dose! And who was he trying to kid? He would come out ahead no matter what happened. In her mind, she couldn't possibly emerge unscathed.

"No way," she reiterated firmly.

"Why not?" he protested. "You've got an entire summer, and you just said you were a good teacher." He picked up her hand and began idly tracing a pattern on it.

"But this is different!" She snatched her hand away. "Loving isn't something you learn to do—it just happens," she informed him exasperatedly. "I can't teach you how to change your attitude, your way of thinking, and frankly, I think that's your problem. I'm a teacher, not a counselor. And besides..." Her jaw closed with a snap. She'd caught herself just in time.

"Besides...what?"

Samantha crossed her arms over her breasts defensively. "Nothing," she muttered. "Just forget it." She looked away from those knowing eyes, aware that they were alight with teasing laughter. What could she say? If she agreed, come September he'd be gone and she'd be left nursing a broken heart? A summer fling with Jason Armstrong might be fun. Fun? It would be heaven itself! But would it be wise? Never!

Jason got to his feet and looked down at her. "Tell me something," he said almost thoughtfully. "Do you ever take any chances? Ever gamble on anything?" When Samantha's jaw tightened, he smiled and looked leisurely around her bedroom, hands on his hips. "I wouldn't be surprised," he continued in the same thoughtful tone, "to find out you bought this house only after inspecting it from stem to stern half a dozen times."

Astute. That's what he was. She had to give him credit for that. Though it was on the tip of her tongue to tell him about her whirlwind romance with Alan six years ago, somehow she had the feeling she'd still end up in the line of fire. But he was right about the house.

Already she could feel a guilty flush creeping up her neck and into her cheeks. She stared straight ahead and refused to look at him. She hated the smile in his voice when he said, "I hit the nail on the head, didn't I?"

"No," she muttered to the wall across from her. "It was only five times—not six."

Jason's laughter followed behind him as he strode across the room to the doorway. "Do me a favor." He turned to face her, an easy smile pulling at his firm lips. "Don't give up on *Love's Sweet Bondage* just yet. Shelve it if you want, but don't pitch it."

Just what on earth was that supposed to mean, Samantha wondered irritably as she clambered out of bed after he had gone.

"Jason Armstrong," she muttered as she shed her nightgown, "you can save your verbal sparring for the worthy opponents in your novels. It's only nine o'clock in the morning and already I feel like I've been through the Hundred Years' War—twice!"

But inside the tiled shower, Samantha found herself admitting that her feelings toward Jason were a muddle of confusion at best. There was no denying the magnetic pull she felt when she was around him. It almost reminded her of the time with Alan, but even then she wasn't sure it had been quite so strong. But feelings of attraction aside, she didn't know if she could even *like* a man whose views on love were so different from her own. Face it, lady, she scolded herself, you're a hopeless romantic, and you'll never be satisfied with a man who isn't the same. And even though Jason wrote the most divine love scenes imaginable, she decided that he probably had no romance left in his soul. Undoubtedly because he poured everything he had into his books, she decided with a rare touch of cynicism.

But dreamer that she was, with the warm steamy water spraying over her body and lulling her into languid complacency, Samantha couldn't help but wonder what it would be like to have Jason Armstrong make love to her. Remembering the exciting warmth of his mouth and the lingering touch of his fingertips against her bare skin sent a fiery throb of awareness pulsing through her veins, making it only too easy to imagine the weight of his hard male body over hers, the heat of his naked skin scorching her own.

She shook her head disgustedly at such brazen thoughts, then laughed as she realized she was chiding herself for her "unseemly" daydreams unnecessarily—exactly as if she was an eighteenth-century maiden instead of a modern woman. Still smiling, she turned off the spray and stepped out of the shower.

"God!"

Samantha whirled in surprise at the sound. Jason stood in the doorway, brown eyes exploring with keen and undeniable male interest the slender lines of her glistening body, still damp with moisture. Stunned by his unexpected appearance, she could only stare at him for what seemed an eternity before grabbing for a towel.

"Damn it, Jason Armstrong!" she sputtered hotly. She fumbled with the ends of the towel as she tried to secure it around her body. "I thought you left!"

"I did." A half-smile tipped his mouth as he stepped forward. "Here, let me." His eyes finally lifted to her face as he deftly tucked the ends of the towel between her breasts, his warm fingers brushing the delicate skin of the valley between.

Annoyed and despising herself for the flush she knew was staining her cheekbones at his intimate touch, as well as for being caught in the nude, she brushed past him into her bedroom. She jerked open a dresser drawer and grabbed a handful of underwear before turning to him.

"Next time you come into my house—or my bathroom," she told him heatedly, "knock!"

"I did." His eyes were full of humor as he watched her stalk to the closet, her jerky movements loosening the dampened towel precariously. "I didn't hear the shower, and when you didn't answer I assumed it was safe to come in. And the door wasn't locked, either."

"I don't usually lock it when I'm here by myself!" she muttered viciously, tugging at the towel and surveying the array of summer clothing. She glanced angrily at Jason, who was leaning against the bathroom doorjamb. His arms were crossed over his chest, and there was an expression of amusement on his handsome face. So he thought she was funny, did he? Well, she'd had enough of him laughing at her. Before the summer was over, the tables would be turned, she vowed silently.

"What do you want this time?" she asked tautly, marching back across the room. She held a brightly colored blouse, which had miraculously survived a vicious yank from the hanger.

He straightened up immediately, his smile fading. "First things first—your mother phoned."

"I'll call her back after I'm dressed," she muttered, more to herself than to him.

"No, you don't need to."

"I don't?" Surprised, she stopped dead in her tracks. Surely her mother hadn't told him not to have her return the call. She never missed a chance to chat—never!

"Uh, no." Did he sound contrite? "She's on the line yet. That's why I came to get you."

"Oh, no!" Samantha dived for the bedside phone. "Why didn't you tell me?"

"I got . . . sidetracked."

An exaggerated leer crossed his face as she glared at him and picked up the receiver. "Hi, mom," she said, forcing a cheery tone, feeling like a volcano about to explode when Jason sat down next to her and ran his fingers caressingly down the side of her arm. "Sorry I took so long, especially when you're calling long-distance." She shot a pointed look at Jason while trying to inch away from his disturbing touch. But with his tall body on one side, the pillow and headboard on the other, she had little leeway.

"That's okay, dear. My nine o'clock appointment canceled at the last minute and my next one isn't until ten." Her mother owned a small beauty shop in Astoria.

"Business good so far this summer?" Samantha aimed a jab at Jason's ribs that he easily parried. His other hand feathered up to her neck and softly stroked the downy skin on her nape.

"Better than last year." Samantha could hear the anxious curiosity mingled with concern in her mother's voice. She anticipated the next question. "Who was the man who answered your phone?"

"A neighbor," she answered quickly, hoping her mother wouldn't think she and Jason... "I, ah, I was outside taking a quick swim. . . ."

"So early in the morning? Wasn't the water awfully cold?"

"Yes . . . cold, very cold, stimulating," she said in a rush, the words tumbling out one after the other. "You know—" she gave a feeble laugh "—it gets the blood going." Why was she the world's worst liar?

"So why wasn't your neighbor in his house instead of yours?"

And why wasn't her mother one to mince words? "He . . . he heard the phone ring while he was passing by. He came to get me . . . which is why it took so long."

"You really should lock your door when you're not home," came her mother's rather dry comment. "Do you know when you'll be coming to visit next?" Her mother continued while Samantha stifled a groan and looked at Jason. "I won't schedule any appointments while you're here. Lana can manage the shop for a week or so if you're planning on staying that long."

Despite the change of subject, Samantha had the distinct impression her mother hadn't believed a word she'd said; it didn't help when Jason's head dipped low to explore the sensitive place where her long neck joined one slender shoulder.

"Will you stop that?" she whispered fiercely, covering the mouthpiece with her hand. His head dropped lower still, and his mouth grazed the rounded tops of her breasts. "You . . . you sex fiend!" she hissed. Her fingers clutched convulsively at the wisp of nylon she still held in her other hand while she tried to ignore the tingle of pleasure racing down her spine.

"What was that, dear?"

"Uh . . . I was just saying . . . I have a friend in Seaside. Maybe I'll stop and see her on my way."

"Seaside? You've never mentioned her before. Who is she?"

Samantha groaned inwardly. If only her mother was a little less on the ball! "She's an old friend from college." She forced a laugh. "I'm sure I've mentioned her. Her name is—" her eyes lit on Jason's book lying on the nightstand "—Cathryn James." Lord, she had better hang up now! She'd find herself in over her head if this call didn't end soon. Thank heaven her mother hadn't picked up a book in years!

"That name does sound familiar, now that I think about it." The soft voice on the other end of the line sounded thoughtful. "Wasn't she your roommate during your freshman year?"

"Uh...yes, that's her. Mom, I really should be g—"

"Very pretty, I recall you saying once, but not terribly bright."

Samantha was sinking ever deeper into a grave of her own digging. She knew she should end this conversation right now, but she couldn't resist a backhanded swipe at Jason. He was watching her with a look that reminded her of a cat stalking a helpless mouse, only he was about to find out that the mouse had the jaws of a lion.

"That's her, mom," she said sweetly, glaring at Jason. "Big on looks, short on brains." At her mother's surprised silence, she amended hastily, "But she really is nice and I—I'm looking forward to seeing her again." At this, Jason, who had been shaking his head, grinned broadly.

"You still haven't told me when you're coming, dear."

"I'm not sure, mom." She glanced acidly at Jason, hardly able to believe he was actually behaving himself, but grateful that the subject of "Cathryn" had been dropped. "Between teaching and working on my house all year, I've hardly had a minute to myself. How about sometime next month?"

"That's fine, Samantha. Try to let me know a few days ahead, though."

"Sure, mom. I'll call you in a few weeks."

The receiver was barely replaced in the cradle when Jason spoke up. "That was quite a performance," he chided mildly. "Do you think she swallowed any of it?"

"Probably not," Samantha answered shortly. "Since I've never lied to my mother before, I'm sure she knows the difference."

"The way you were hem-hawing around, I wouldn't be at all surprised." He raised an eyebrow. "Why didn't you tell her the truth about why I was here?"

Samantha was already feeling enough guilt without Jason adding to it. "The truth?" she snapped. "That we've known each other less than a day and already you're coming and going from my house exactly as you please? If you'll recall, I didn't know why you came back again—and I still don't!"

Jason merely smiled at her, clearly not at all disturbed by her anger. "I'm not sure you want to know right now," he murmured, rising lithely to his feet.

"You're right—I don't!" She pointed at the bedroom door, still standing ajar. "I think you've overstayed your welcome."

He wasted no time in pouncing. "So you *were* glad to see me."

"Of course I wasn't!" When was she going to remember that this man made a living juggling words? She was going to have to watch what she said around him.

"Not even a little?"

The little-boy plaintiveness in his voice, whether feigned or real, reminded her for all the world of one of her second-graders. She felt her heart doing strange things in her chest. "Well...maybe a little," she relented cautiously. Jason Armstrong was impossible— irresistible! And she was a fool. There was no way someone as average in looks and manner as she was could ever hope to land a man like Jason Armstrong. Given his casual outlook on love, the odds for any woman were probably a million to one.

But to her surprise, and then growing delight, he bent over and kissed her again, lightly at first and then with increasing urgency. His hands framed the oval of her face, and Samantha was aware of a yawning chasm of desire spreading through her body.

"Say yes," Jason murmured against her mouth, his tongue tracing the outline of her lips with moist sensuous strokes. "Yes..."

All pretense of thought had long since vanished under the onslaught of his touch. Samantha lifted heavy eyelids to gaze up at him longingly. "Yes," she whispered in husky compliance, vaguely hoping he would continue this passionate assault on her senses. Her lashes drifted closed again.

A low laugh of satisfaction vibrated against her cheek. "I knew it." There was a kind of pleased self-complacency in his voice as his breath fanned her skin. "I knew I could get you to say yes." One last kiss against the corner of her mouth and Samantha was deprived of his vital male warmth. "Remember, seven o'clock tonight at my place."

At his abrupt withdrawal, her eyes flew open and she was brought to an almost painful awareness. She tugged at her rapidly slipping towel. "Wait!" she cried, seeing that Jason's long strides had already taken him halfway across the room. "Seven o'clock at your place...for what?" Dear Lord, what had she done? He could have demanded anything...

anything! And after a taste of his abundant male charms, she realized that *anything* could very well turn out to be *everything*.

He paused at the doorway, one hand curled around the knob as he gave her a lazy smile. "Second thoughts already? I can guarantee you won't be disappointed."

That was exactly what she was afraid of. She swallowed nervously. "Disappointed in what?"

Jason shook his head, brown eyes glinting teasingly. "My, my," he admonished gently. "You'd make a terrible businesswoman. Don't you know you shouldn't sign your life away without first finding out the terms of the agreement?"

"Terms, nothing!" she sputtered. She was becoming a little annoyed with his deliberately evasive tactics. "All I want to know is what I'm in for tonight—*if* I decide to show up!"

"Oh, you will," he assured her smugly. He leaned against the door frame. "And you can expect delight and pleasure far surpassing anything you've ever known before." At her indignant gasp he continued as if he hadn't heard her, the firm lines of his mouth still turned up in that infuriatingly confident smile. "Something to tempt your awareness, whet your appetite, a total seduction of the senses...."

"No." Samantha shook her head. She took a deep breath, trying to ignore the nagging feeling of disappointment rising within her. Jason Armstrong might take such things lightly, but she was one person who couldn't discard the principles of a lifetime for one fleeting moment of pleasure.

She looked up and met his gaze unflinchingly. "Let's get one thing straight," she said clearly. "I'm not coming—"

"You don't know what you'll be missing," he interrupted in a mocking tone that set Samantha's teeth on edge. "My lasagna is the best in the west. Are you sure—"

"Of course I'm sure!" she snapped. "I won't be there tonight and that's fi—" She stopped as his words finally sank in. "Lasagna?" she asked tentatively. "All that talk about temptation and seduction, and you were asking me for dinner?" At his nod, she bit her lip and laughed shakily. "Oh, dear, and I thought..." Her voice trailed off. She met his eyes hesitantly but dropped her gaze almost immediately.

"You have an overactive imagination, young lady. Probably comes from reading too many romance novels." There was a tiny rustle of movement as he straightened his long body. "I'll see you tonight."

Samantha looked up suddenly. "But I haven't said I'll co—"

"Oh, yes, you did," he reminded her smoothly. He reached again for the doorknob. "And surely you wouldn't deprive a man of a mere few hours of female companionship, would you? Not when he's direly in need of a pleasure-filled evening. I'd even go so far as to say he's starving for a woman's company."

"Starving!" Her eyes opened wide in disbelief. "Yesterday you were practically bragging about your experience with women, and now you're trying to tell me you need a woman—"

"But not just any woman," he cut in with a devastating smile that sent Samantha's blood pounding frantically along her veins. "Not just any woman," he repeated softly. There was a husky timbre in his voice that played across her skin, sending shivers of excitement through her body. "You... only you."

Jason's eyes impaled hers with gentle scrutiny from across the room. Samantha found she couldn't look away from those warm brown depths or the quiet intensity in his lean features, which, for once, bore no trace of laughter.

She shifted uncertainly, still perched on the edge of her unmade bed. His teasing remarks and gentle mockery were easier to deal with. At least then she could shield herself with a wall of annoyance and resentment. Did Jason Armstrong, with his glib and honeyed tongue, somehow present a threat to her rather staid existence?

He was exactly like the heroes in his books—strong, dynamic, a man who could take charge of any situation and come out on top.

Yet somehow she suspected that she was the one who had emerged the victor in their little skirmish yesterday, at least in Jason's eyes, but not without sustaining a loss of her own. Her gaze slid away from Jason's to linger on the copy of *Love's Sweet Bondage*. A touch of wistfulness mingled with the almost poignant look in her eyes.

"I'll see you tonight," Jason repeated. Suddenly she knew that the choice, if it had ever been hers in the first place, had already been made for her. Aware that her silence affirmed her concurrence, she felt her heart thud heavily in her chest as he gave her another long slow look before stepping into the hallway. Once there, he stopped and looked over his shoulder, and it irked her for some reason to see the familiar teasing glint back in his eyes.

"By the way," he said with a wink, "I love your underwear."

His eyes dropped meaningfully to her lap. She looked down in puzzlement to find she still clutched the small scrap of cloth she had snatched from her dresser—it seemed like eons ago. To her horror, she discovered the tiny white bikini underpants were liberally dotted with shiny bright-red hearts, each one pierced with an arrow from Cupid's bow.

Embarrassment at having kept the silly gag gift from her mother, who was well acquainted with her daughter's penchant for romantic novels, was suddenly turned into anger at Jason, who seemed to have an uncanny knack for catching her in the most ridiculous situations.

"I won't be there tonight," she yelled after his departing figure.

"Yes, you will," he called back in a tone of supreme confidence. "I'm fixing dinner for two and I hate leftovers."

"That's your problem, not mine!" she shouted. She was determined not to let him get the best of her.

She heard the low rumble of his laughter somewhere in the vicinity of her kitchen, followed by the screen door slamming against the wooden frame.

Samantha gave a sigh of sheer exasperation, but smiled to herself a moment later. No doubt Jason thought he could twist her around his little finger with ludicrous ease, but he would soon learn differently. He hated leftovers? Well, she would show him! He'd simply have to stuff himself until he resembled an overgrown cabbage, because there was no way on earth she was going to have dinner with him that night!

Four

Samantha's mind hadn't changed when a knock on her front door announced a caller later that morning. She scowled as she opened it, half expecting Jason to be standing on her doorstep with that maddening grin plastered on his face.

Instead she found a gum-popping, fresh-faced teenager. "This 145 Shoreline Street?" he asked, shifting both sneakered feet.

She eyed him rather dubiously. "Yes."

"Got a delivery for ya." He gestured to someone behind him and opened the screen door wide.

Samantha watched openmouthed as another teenager maneuvered a huge carton past her through the doorway. "Where do you want this, lady?" the first one asked.

Her confused eyes fixed on the other young man, who had lifted the carton with ridiculous ease despite its bulk and was awaiting her instruction. "Why, there must be some mistake. I haven't bought anything—"

"You Samantha Monroe?" He pulled a frazzled-looking piece of paper from his pocket.

She looked at the van parked in the driveway. It bore the name of a novelty shop in Lincoln City. "Yes, but—"

"Got the order right here. This is supposed to go to Samantha Monroe."

"I don't understand. Surely there must be..."

Her protest fell on deaf ears as he turned and headed out the door, calling back over his shoulder, "Come on, Bill, let's get the rest." The second young man finally deposited the box in the entryway and followed him out.

"The rest" turned out to be three more boxes exactly like the first. Feeling rather dazed, Samantha shouldered her way between the waist-high boxes, then hesitantly lifted one. It was light, lighter than she had expected. Could it possibly be empty? She eyed it uncertainly. If she hadn't ordered this, someone else must have... Jason. It had to be Jason. Her mouth turned down at the corners. What a prank!

She ripped open the first box with a vengeance, but her battle-cry turned into a gasp when she parted the cardboard flaps. Dozens of bright shiny balloons floated upward from their nest.

She was speechless by the time she opened the last of the cartons. She stepped back to survey the sight. The ceiling of her tiny dining room was canopied with an array of wall-to-wall balloons, suspended by gaily colored ribbons and tied together in bunches of three. There was every color imaginable—ruby-red, bright pink, lavender, violet—and all in the shape of a heart. She couldn't help but smile at the hot-pink lettering emblazoned across the shiny surface of one balloon—Do You Kiss and Tell? Another read Embrace Me; still another Be Mine.

She tugged playfully at a ribbon, watching as it drifted upward. It was then that she noticed a card attached to one. Her fingers weren't entirely steady as she slipped the card from the envelope, and she couldn't stop the warmth that flooded her when she read the message. *As one heartthrob might say to another, my heart beats only for you.* It was no surprise to find Jason's name scrawled at the bottom.

Maybe it was mere curiosity that made her decide, almost in spite of herself, that it wouldn't hurt to get to know Jason better. Yet somehow she didn't think it was. Later she found herself rationalizing that it wasn't every day she had the chance to rub elbows with a famous author. Or possibly, if she was honest with herself, it was simply the sheer magnetism of the man.

Certainly she had to admit to being touched. No one had ever sent her a roomful of balloons before!

Whatever the reason, seven o'clock that evening found Samantha critically studying her reflection in front of the mirror. The pale yellow of the peasant-style dress she wore set off the light tan she'd acquired during her two days of sunbathing. The boatneck styling of the dress was off the shoulder, and her smooth skin gleamed in the waning beams of sunlight that lit her bedroom. But she despaired at the sight of her sunburned nose, which neither makeup nor powder toned down more than a shade. Never before had she minded quite so much that she didn't possess fashion model prettiness. Suddenly she found herself yearning for a bit more in the way of looks and body or, barring that, a dash of worldly sophistication. Was that the kind of woman Jason was usually drawn to?

When she realized what she was doing she frowned. Somehow she just couldn't shake the image of Jason with a pair of extremely well-endowed California beauties on each arm. Why take such pains over her appearance? She could never even hope to compete against women like that, and there was no use trying.

With a sigh she picked up a delicately crocheted shawl and headed for the door. "If it's a pinup girl you're after, Jason Armstrong," she grumbled as she left the house, "you'd better head back to Tinseltown. And if you have any complaints, you'd better keep them to yourself, because I won't hesitate to remind you this whole thing was your idea!"

Five minutes later, Samantha was standing on Jason's doorstep. Despite the sun's presence in the western sky, the temperature had dropped drastically in the late afternoon in typically unpredictable Oregon fashion. She shivered as she lifted a finger to the doorbell.

Jason opened the door wide, and Samantha's eyes met his with an unspoken challenge. She half expected him to laugh and say, "I knew you didn't mean it! Didn't I tell you you'd show up?" But all he murmured as he ushered her inside was, "Right on time, I see."

Samantha looked around the living room appreciatively as he took her shawl, admiring the contemporary style so different from her own cozy dwelling. The floor plan was open and spacious, the sloped ceiling warmed by a massive stone fireplace. Across the room, sliding glass doors opened onto a balcony and deck.

Jason reappeared, a half-smile tipping his mouth as he stood before her. A decided gleam in his eyes, he took in every aspect of her figure. "Nice dress, Samantha," he murmured warmly. "You look—" his eyes reassessed her body "—almost as good with your clothes on as you do with them off." His smile widened as his eyes returned to her face. "Sunburned nose and all."

Samantha reddened. He didn't have to make her feel like Bozo the Clown! "I could say the same of you!" she shot back hotly. He was dressed in a pale gray shirt and dark slacks, the first time she'd seen him in anything but just shorts. Too late she realized what she had said.

He laughed. "But you haven't seen me with my clothes off yet, have you?"

She felt like turning tail and running the other way. When was she going to learn? She didn't dare say anything in front of this man! "Close enough," she muttered. "Close enough."

Jason only laughed again. "Come help me with the salad," he suggested, catching her hand in his and leading her toward the kitchen.

Moments later, he had armed her with a stainless steel bowl and a small paring knife. "Did you tell me yesterday how long you've lived here?" he questioned as he opened the refrigerator. "I don't remember."

Samantha eyed him rather warily, half-afraid to open her mouth. Was it any wonder she had the feeling he would make mincemeat of anything she said? She began to meticulously peel a cucumber. "I've taught here for two years, but I bought my house last summer."

"You said your mother called long-distance," he recalled. "Where does she live?"

"Astoria."

He pulled two wineglasses from the cupboard and paused to look at her. "So that's where you're from originally?"

She hesitated, then shook her head.

Jason eyed her across the cutting board. "You're just a bundle of information, aren't you?" he chided with a laugh. "Don't be so modest." He gave her an encouraging smile and began shredding lettuce into the bowl. "How do you think I come up with ideas for the characters in my books? Let me pick your brains. Who knows? Maybe you'll show up in the next one."

Her? Now that was a laugh. His heroines were known for their feistiness, their fiery tempers and vivacity, their ability to take someone in hand and whip him into shape—except the hero, of course. Was that why she liked his heroines so much, because they were all the things she wasn't, but secretly longed to be?

She smiled in spite of herself. She wasn't sure she'd want to change even if she could. "Not a chance."

"Oh, come on." Jason's tone was cajoling. "So what if you're not a woman with a past?" He tipped his head to the side and smiled engagingly, while eyeing her a bit quizzically. "If you're not originally from Astoria, where *are* you from?"

Samantha gave in with a sigh. This was a man who could probably charm a pirate into walking the plank—ever so willingly. "I was born in Kansas City, Missouri," she finally told him.

He nodded. "And raised there, too, I'll bet—" He stopped when she smilingly shook her head. "No? Well, then, spit it out! Where were you raised?"

A smile curved her lips. "Here, there and everywhere," she murmured lightly.

Jason stopped his shredding long enough to survey her with a curious squint. "Where—exactly?"

She began to slice the cucumber into the bowl, took a deep breath and began her spiel. "Toledo, Ohio; Lincoln, Nebraska; Reno, Nevada; Billings, Montana; Evansville, Indiana; Waco, Texas; Flagstaff, Arizona; Oshkosh, Wiscon—"

"Whoa, slow down!" He eyed her in disbelief. "You're not serious!"

"Oh, but I am." Her lashes shielding her eyes, she continued her slicing. "And all before the age of twelve." Though the memory wasn't what she would call welcome, she kept her smile firmly glued in place. "But at least I can say I've been relatively stable the last few years. I've stayed in the same state, and any move I made was my choice."

There was an empty silence. Samantha could feel Jason's eyes on her but didn't look up. He'd wanted to know—well, now he did. "Don't tell me," he said slowly, "your father was a pilot who decided to move his family along with every flight."

"For all I know, he could be by now." Her light tone wasn't at all in keeping with the dark shadow of memory creeping over her. "It would be the perfect job for dear old dad."

Gentle fingers firmly removed the knife from her grasp. Jason took her by the shoulders and raised her chin with a finger. "Not a pleasant childhood, I presume?"

Samantha reluctantly met his eyes. If he laughed at her now! "It had its moments," she admitted a bit grudgingly. All too few, though. She'd hated being constantly on the move; it seemed she had no more than gotten settled in school when her father was yanking her out. She'd soon learned there was little point in making friends; she wouldn't be there long enough to keep them before her father uprooted his family once again in search of another harebrained scheme. Real estate ventures, restaurant partnerships, car sales . . . too many jobs to count. "It's the opportunity of a lifetime," he'd always proclaimed enthusiastically. And so it was . . . until the next one came along.

Jason's voice was strangely gentle. "You haven't seen your father in quite some time?"

Fourteen years. Yes, that was quite some time. Her lashes dropped and she nodded.

"What happened?" There was a kind of gentle insistence in his voice.

"Can't you tell? I'm the product of a broken home," she responded lightly. And a broken marriage. She pushed the thought aside. "My parents divorced after—after dear old dad faded into the sunset one day." She shrugged and turned her lips up in an artificial smile, trying to shake the sudden dark mood. Gently disengaging herself from Jason's grip, she began to toss the salad. "What about you?" she asked with false brightness. "Any ghosts lurking in your past?"

There was an instant's silence. He took the hint and moved away, searching in the drawer for a pair of hot mitts. "None that you'd be interested in," he finally responded. He pressed a warm kiss on the back of her neck before turning to the oven.

"Unfair," Samantha objected, ignoring the sudden lurch of her heart at his touch. He turned around, a steaming dish in his hands. She picked up the salad bowl and followed him into the dining room. "That's an evasive answer if ever I've heard one."

Jason merely shrugged and set the dish on a trivet in the center of the table. It was elegantly set, complete with gleaming crystal and china, linen tablecloth and napkin. Before they sat down, he dimmed the lights and struck a match to the slender taper in the center of the table.

In spite of the disturbing conversation about her father, Samantha found herself relaxing. The talk between them was light and sporadic but altogether comfortable. It wasn't until they had both finished eating that he pushed aside their plates and caught her eye, his brown eyes gleaming.

"Well, did I lie?"

Samantha eyed him over the flickering flame of the candle. "About what?"

He sighed. "My lasagna—best in the west. How was it?"

She laughed, unable to stop herself. The sauce had been rich, meaty and flavorful, seasoned with fresh herbs and spices. It had been delicious. The salad, too, had been light and crisp, the flavor enhanced by the dressing Jason claimed to have stirred up himself. It had been a perfect meal. "It was fantastic," she said warmly. "Everything you said and more."

"At last a woman who appreciates the finer things in life." His eyes met hers across the table, warm and glowing, and Samantha was reminded of that gentle kiss on her nape. A sudden heat warmed her body.

She took a nervous sip of the full-bodied red wine he'd served with the meal. "Where did you learn to cook like that?"

"My parents have an Italian restaurant in Los Angeles. My mother makes the pasta, my father the sauce."

She looked up with interest. "Any brothers or sisters?"

Jason nodded his head good-naturedly. "Two older sisters. When I was growing up, I never knew if I was supposed to play with dolls or trucks."

A tiny smile curved her lips as she eyed him beneath half-closed lids. He was leaning back in his chair and smiling across at her. The smile lines around his eyes and near his mouth were oddly appealing. His shirt was open at the throat, revealing a tangle of crisp curling hairs. He'd rolled the sleeves up to his elbows, and her eyes lingered on those muscular forearms. Her pulse skitterd alarmingly and she stifled an odd feeling in the pit of her stomach. No, living with two sisters had certainly never had the slightest effect on his masculinity. He was as intensely virile as any man she had ever met—either in the flesh or between the pages of a book!

"You know, I think my mother would like you."

Samantha's eyes flew up to his. "Would she?"

"I know she would. There's a lot to like." His voice was undeniably warm, but Samantha felt her cheeks color slightly. She wasn't quite sure how to take the remark. Did he mean inside or outside? Surely not outside. She was an average American female—in looks, manner and every other way. The type of woman a man wouldn't mind taking home to his mother, the type who would never pose a threat to another woman, be it mother, sister or lover. She'd never minded before. Why was she suddenly wishing for cover-girl looks?

The answer was sitting across from her in the form of an undeniably attractive man, a man who could probably have any woman of his choosing. So what was he doing here with an ordinary-looking nobody like her?

She cleared her throat and traced a finger around the rim of her glass. "How long did you say you'd be staying?"

"Here in Neskowin?"

"Yes."

"Most of the summer, I imagine." He shrugged. "However the mood strikes me."

Somehow that grated against her, but she ignored it. "You mentioned yesterday that this was a working vacation—you're writing another book?"

He nodded and pushed back his chair, then came to her and pulled her to her feet. "Not that I'm trying to change the subject, but I hope you weren't counting on dessert. It completely slipped my mind." He gave a gentle tug on both her hands and drew her a step closer. "Unless you don't mind a substitute?"

Samantha's gaze focused on the strongly beating pulse in his throat, faintly obscured by bristly dark hairs. Something in his tone brought her eyes to his in a flash. She moistened suddenly dry lips with the tip of her tongue. "I have the feeling this is the male version of coffee, tea or me."

A slow smile spread across his lean features. His eyes followed the movement of her tongue on its unconsciously provocative path around her mouth. "You're a perceptive woman, Samantha Monroe," he said softly.

A blatant invitation to his bed couldn't have been more clear. Something leaped inside her for a second but she stilled the wild impulse and deliberately chose to misunderstand. She looked quickly away. "That's a tall order," she said lightly. "A little too tall for my tastes."

Jason shrugged his wide shoulders. "Only if you make it that way."

Samantha swallowed. Her eyes slid back to his face. "I—I thought we settled this yesterday."

"And I thought maybe you'd had a change of heart."

His easy smile pulled at her heartstrings, but she tugged her hands free. "We just met yesterday," she began uncertainly, wishing she could be more sure of him—and herself, as well. "We really shouldn't—"

His hearty chuckle pulled her up short. "Ever the soul of discretion, aren't you?" He wrapped an arm around her shoulders and hugged her to him tightly. "Just kidding, Samantha," he said with a soft laugh. "Just kidding."

But moments later she wasn't so sure. Samantha found herself drawn along with him to the wide expanse of glass facing the ocean. The sun was a fiery ball of orange as it prepared to slip below the horizon. The endless sheet of water was bathed in a shimmering shade of amber and gold. Wispy clouds tinged with lavender and pink lay just above the surface.

"Made to order just for us, wasn't it?"

Samantha made no comment, barely able to breathe for the warmth of the muscular arm still wrapped around her.

"The view is even better from upstairs."

His fingers burned a fiery imprint into her upper arms. She swallowed. "Is—is it?" was all she could manage from the tight knot of awareness in her throat.

"Mmm." A warm mouth brushed her temple.

"From . . . the bedroom, I suppose." That whisper of sound—was it really hers?

"As a matter of fact, yes. We could watch that mystical moment when the sun falls below the earth, and sun-warmed day becomes moon-kissed night..." It would have sounded corny coming from anyone else's lips. Something jangled in her brain, but all she could focus on was the sensual magic of his voice. "All totally innocuous, of course." That voice was now wrapped in laughter. Did she only imagine the hint of velvet beneath? Wishful thinking perhaps?

Ever so gently Jason turned her to face him. Samantha gazed up into his face, those lean features almost tender. Those warm, brown eyes were the shade of chocolate and just as addictive.

"Of course," she echoed calmly, pulling away and retreating a few steps. Her eyes swept around the room as if seeking an escape, stopping on the table, which hadn't yet been cleared. It was there that she directed her steps, gathering up the plates and empty casserole dish.

Jason trailed along behind her, glasses and cutlery in hand. "Something tells me I've just made a fatal faux pas," he said, casting a look at her from the corner of his eye. "Are you telling me my efforts to please were all in vain?"

A ghost of a smile hovered on her lips at his valiant attempt to try to look wounded. She emptied her armload onto the kitchen counter. "Not exactly," she conceded in a carefully neutral tone.

He raised both eyebrows in a silent question.

Samantha made a vague gesture with one hand. It was clear that the entire atmosphere he'd created—the wine, the food, the candlelight—was entirely for her benefit. Was their disturbing exchange yesterday afternoon and his ultimate challenge to her this morning behind it? What was it he'd said? Give me an education. Show me how wrong I am about love. Well, who wouldn't be impressed by such an effort? It was designed to appeal to a woman's romantic soul, and wasn't hers more romantic than most?

She couldn't help but wonder if he was the one trying to teach her a lesson. Even more importantly, if they hadn't had that disturbing conversation, would he have put himself out? For another woman he was trying to lure into his bed perhaps, but for *her?*

On second thought, she wasn't sure she wanted to know.

"I really am flattered, Jason." At least I think I am. "But it's just that..." She stopped, unsure of what she wanted to say.

He gave her an engaging smile, his teeth very white against his tan.

"Well..." Damn! Why did he have to smile like that now? It made her legs feel like melting wax. "The wine, the candlelight—" all that he had done drifted into her mind "—the dinner and the..." The balloons! She'd completely forgotten about them. Small wonder, when one was faced with a man like Jason Armstrong. What was a houseful of balloons compared to a face and body like his?

Jason laughed at her sudden stricken look. "You did get my present?" he inquired blandly.

"I... yes. Yes, and they're really very precious! In fact, it looks like you bought out an entire store..." She was rattling, he'd think she was a complete idiot! A simple thank-you would have sufficed, wouldn't it? "I... Thank you. Thank you so much," she finally finished hurriedly.

"After seeing your underwear this morning, I thought you might fancy Valentine's Day in June." A warm smile curved his lips, and he calmly led her into the living room and seated her on the low-slung leather couch in front of the fireplace. Her head still whirling, Samantha watched as he turned away to strike a match to the kindling and cedar logs already in place in the grate. Orange-tipped flames licked upward. Once again, something prodded at her brain, just out of reach.

Jason sat down beside her and slipped a long arm along the back of the couch so that his fingertips lay nearly touching the bare skin of her upper arm. "Now," he began lightly, "you were saying?"

Samantha frowned as he sat down beside her. "About tonight," he prodded gently. "All my wasted efforts..."

She cleared her throat. "Yes, well—"

"Wait! Don't start yet—I'll be back in just a minute!" Jason suddenly jumped up and strode into the kitchen, coming back with two more glasses of wine. He set them on the raised hearth, extinguished the single lamp that burned on the end table so that the only light came from a dim lamp burning in a corner of the dining room, then switched on the stereo and tuned in some soft background music. Finally he pulled her down onto the plush carpet in front of the fireplace.

"Jason—" A protest hovered on her lips as he pressed a glass into her hand and joined her on the floor. He'd refilled her glass frequently during dinner and she was beginning to feel the effects. She looked at him suspiciously. "Are you trying to get the two of us drunk?"

"Not to worry." He broke into an audacious grin. "Alcohol affects a man's ability—don't you remember? You pointed that out just yesterday."

"It's supposed to affect his performance—not his ability!" Sitting up straight, she inched back from him, arranged her skirt over her knees and darted him an indignant glance. "And I distinctly remember you telling me that you've never had that problem!"

He shrugged and leaned back against the hearth. "Always a first time, always a first time." Looking wholly innocent, he patted the spot beside him. "Why don't you come and sit by the fire? If it doesn't keep you warm, I think I can manage."

She glared at him. "Jason Armstrong, you just never quit, do you? I'm beginning to think you have a serious problem with the word 'no.'"

"Funny, I don't remember you saying that."

Samantha ignored him. "And furthermore," she continued hotly, "it's as plain as the nose on your face—"

"Whose?" He stared pointedly at the sunburned tip of her nose.

She said a silent prayer and counted to twenty. "And furthermore," she reiterated, "it's as plain as the nose on *your* face that the dinner and the music are all part of a little planned seduction scene on your part." Suddenly she stopped. That elusive something that had been dancing around in her brain the last few minutes was back again.

"Wait a minute," she breathed. "Wait just a minute. What you said before... about watching the sunset..." She snapped her fingers and began to quote. "'We could watch that mystical moment when the sun goes down and...'"

"And sun-warmed day becomes moon-kissed night," he finished, a triumphant gleam in his eye.

Samantha jerked upright to her knees. "You used that line in *Midnight Enchantment*! That's what Beau said to Pauline the first time they—" Her mouth clamped shut and an angry finger sliced through the air. It was the same—almost exactly! Both fists landed on her slim hips. "He set her up! He knew she'd never be able to say no once he turned on the charm! He had everything planned—right down to the sheets on the bed!''

Jason lifted his glass in a silent toast. "You see why females were known as the weaker sex in those days," he said mildly. "Pauline deserved what she got, to say nothing of wanting it. She was trying to blackmail him into marriage."

"Beau was a scoundrel—especially at first! And Pauline only did it to save her family!"

Jason sighed. "Oh, yes, those southern belles. Noble if not wise." His brown eyes crinkled as he looked at her. "But if you'll recall, they didn't end up using the bed."

"Is that why you dragged me down in front of the fireplace?" His smile set her teeth on edge. "I can't believe it! Your own private version of *Midnight Enchantment*! Dammit, how could you?"

"I couldn't resist." He shrugged, sending her a teasing smile. "My heroes get to have all the fun and I have to do all the work."

And he thought she was ripe for the taking? Samantha seethed. "I suppose if I checked the bed I'd find satin sheets?"

Jason snapped his fingers. "Darn! I knew I forgot something. Beau had a lot of trouble smuggling crimson satin sheets through the blockade." One corner of his mouth turned up ruefully. "I don't have any excuse, though. I guess I should have borrowed your copy and checked." Looking up at her, he smiled apologetically. "I suppose that means you're safe for tonight. My heroes might be rather unscrupulous, but I'm not."

Samantha snorted. "That's a joke! Your heroes might be unscrupulous at times but at least they have a heart—"

"Even Beau?"

"Even Beau." She eyed his loose-limbed form, now stretched out lazily on the carpet, his dark head propped against his hand. "Especially Beau! I'm not so sure about you!"

Jason lifted himself to a sitting position, long legs tucked up in front of his chest. "Wow!" he said softly. "You've really got it in for me! I guess I'm going to have to change while I'm here."

"As the saying goes, if it ain't broke, don't fix it! You keep telling me you're in perfect working order, so why bother?" She turned and would have flounced from the room but suddenly Jason was there before her. She hadn't known he could move that fast.

"Well, then . . . couldn't we use a bandage?"

Samantha looked up to find a hopeful expression on his face, but his eyes were dancing with devilry. She suddenly realized he had cupped her shoulders in his hands and was gently running his fingertips over the bare skin of her arms. An occasional finger trespassed into the sleeve of her dress.

"Fine," she muttered. "You do that." But the words lacked their former heat. Already she was weakening. She was beginning to suspect that staying angry with this man was indeed a lost cause.

And that was her last thought for a very long time. His mouth came down on hers, hard and tender, inviting and demanding. Samantha felt something inside her blossom and grow, something she hadn't felt in years—something she'd never felt before. She shivered when his mouth left hers to blaze a trail of fire down the slender column of her neck to the wildly beating pulse throbbing in her throat.

Her body was lifted and fitted even more closely against his unyielding bulk. Never before had she felt so helpless, so much a puppet in the hands of a master, but she couldn't have cared less. She felt a sensation not unlike a feather drifting slowly down to earth, unaware that she'd been swept from her feet and borne downward until she felt the plushness of the sofa at her back.

"God, you're sweet." Jason's groan was muffled against her parted lips. "And soft...I've never touched anyone so soft...."

Samantha opened her eyes to stare at the dark face hovering just above hers. The shooting flames of the fire cast flickering shadows over his lean features, throwing into prominence his straight nose and full sensuous mouth. Driven by some need she didn't fully understand, she lifted a hand to him.

"You don't have to say that." Her fingers came in contact with his lower lip, trembling slightly as they traced the shape of it. "You don't h—"

His mouth opened to nip gently at her fingertips while long fingers tangled in her hair and pulled her mouth to his. His lips swallowed her halting whisper. His laugh was a little shaky when he finally drew away. "Yes, I do. I want to." He gave her another lingering kiss. "Don't you know that?"

"Jason..." His name was a whisper, a prayer, a demand and a plea. His response was all she had ever dreamed of and more. His fingers caressed and explored, glided and probed. She moaned as he turned so that they lay facing each other, their legs entwined together. She ached to feel his touch on her bare skin and arched against him in an effort to make known her silent plea, delighting in the bold thrust that surged against her.

Aching desire rippled through her body, so strong it almost shocked her. She was on fire, naked flames of longing sizzling through her blood. Jason Armstrong was all that she had ever wanted in a man, all that she needed, all she had ever dreamed of. He was a renegade, an outlaw, and she was his prey; a brigand and a pirate, and she was his booty, his prize. He was a wealthy sea captain, a mighty landowner and she was his mistress, his beloved bride and his most treasured possession. She was the woman who could tame all of those men and gain a world in the bargain. He was the dream lover she had always yearned for, the tender suitor whose arms would shield and protect her forever.

He invited and she gave; she yielded and he took; he dominated and she controlled. And all the while, her mind was carrying her farther and farther away, to a place she'd never been before, a place that existed only in the mind—a Garden of Eden, a castle in the air. But the pleasure his roaming hands gave was only too real, the warm breath filling her mouth and fanning her skin all too tangible.

It no longer mattered that this was a stage supplied by Jason; the wine, the fire, the moonlight streaming through the windows and bathing the room in a silver glow, nothing but props. Never before had Samantha felt so alive and so vital, or so wanted. Wanted by the man above her. He was Beau. He was Marshall. He was a dozen other imaginary heroes all rolled into one, the man she'd always wanted but could never have. He was the most exciting man on this earth and he wanted her.

She moaned, a tiny sound of protest. Her fingers were curled in the silky mat of hair on his abdomen, his skin was warm and faintly damp. Their clothes were a barrier she could no longer tolerate. Her eyes opened, dazed and pleasure-filled, and her fingers began to fumble with the buttons of his shirt. Jason's eyes opened, too, and he smiled into hers. The smoldering warmth she saw there sent a rush of pleasure surging through her body, and she took a deep breath to clear her swelling senses. The heady scent of his after-shave filled her nostrils as she lifted her head and teasingly brushed her mouth across his, but suddenly she froze.

She sat up, blue eyes wide and dazed as they swept around the room. She sniffed, and sniffed again. Then her mouth opened in a soundless scream.

"Fire!" she managed to gasp. *"Fire!"*

Five

Samantha finally pointed an arm toward the fire-place. Through the wire-mesh screen, flames could be seen licking eagerly upward. Jason jumped up from the couch and stared across the room. His eyes opened wide, his jaw dropped open and he stood rooted to the floor as if he was cemented in place.

"For God's sake!" Samantha dove across the floor. Ghostly billows of smoke climbed toward the ceiling. Grabbing the poker from the set of brass-finished tools on the hearth, she shoved it inside the screen and searched frantically for the handle of the damper. When it was finally opened, she threw open the windows and pushed aside the sliding glass door.

Jason still stood where she'd left him. His jaw had finally closed, but there was a stupefied look in his eyes as they moved disbelievingly from the fireplace to where Samantha stood with her hands on her hips.

She'd adjusted her dress while opening the windows, but Jason's partially unbuttoned shirt hung half in and half out of his slacks. His fingers had carved half a dozen pathways through his dark hair. Gone was the dashing and debonair soul of an hour before. But despite his rumpled appearance, he still looked damnably good to her.

She wasn't sure how welcome the admission was, because in the face of her near surrender, she realized there would have been no stopping either one of them in only a few short minutes. An unwilling smile tugged at her lips. Jason Armstrong had almost killed them both—well, perhaps that was an exaggeration. But she could imagine the headlines of the weekly Lincoln City newspaper. *Neskowin Lovers Succumb to Smoke.* And to think she was worried about succumbing to *him!*

It was her outright giggle that finally penetrated his dazed state. "What's so funny?" he growled. He finally moved to take her arm and pull her into the dining room.

"You," she said brashly. "Don't you know you're supposed to open the damper before you start a fire? But then I guess you wouldn't—" she grinned impishly "—coming from Southern California. You must worry more about how to keep cool than how to keep warm."

Jason scowled. "I forgot about it." He stared at her a second before a reluctant smile tugged at his lips. "I guess I should be glad you smelled the smoke before it did any real damage. I don't think David would be very happy if I told him I almost managed to burn down his house."

At the mention of his friend, Samantha's smile faded. It was an almost unwelcome reminder that Jason's appearance in her life was only temporary. She would never see him again after this summer, and it was altogether possible he wouldn't be staying that long.

Heaving an inward sigh, she made a move toward the entryway but Jason stopped her.

"You're not leaving yet, are you?"

She hesitated. Much as she hated to admit it, this was no more than a game to him. Love was probably a game to him, he'd as much as said so yesterday. And yet his devilishly handsome features touched something inside her that made her want desperately to throw caution to the winds and let the magic flow. Hard to believe of a woman who meticulously planned even her meals a month in advance.

Her hair swirled gently on her cheek as she shook her head. She softened her words with a slightly wistful smile. "I think I'd better."

His self-assured air was back in full force and running full speed ahead. "Why? 'The night is still young,'" he quoted in a deep velvet tone, "'and who knows what untold pleasures await the two of us?'"

Samantha cast a wary eye in his direction and stepped to the front door. "The only pleasure that awaits me is the pleasure of my bed—" she squelched the hopeful gleam in his eye with a look and a word "—*alone*."

He leaned against the door frame and smiled. "Saved not by the bell," he quipped softly, "but by the fire."

Samantha couldn't hold back a laugh. He might be persistent but at least he conceded defeat gracefully. "You can let this place air out while you walk me home," she told him as he draped her shawl around her shoulders.

A salt-tanged breeze curled around their silent figures as they walked the narrow pathway between the
two houses. A full moon spilled down from the sky,
lighting the way. Samantha stopped once to shake
sand out of her sandal.

"This is one of the pitfalls of living on the beach in
the summer," she said with a laugh as she slipped it
off. Jason obligingly bent down so she could prop her
hand on his back while she hopped on one foot. "You
see why I have a hose outside my back door?"

"You really love it here, don't you." It was more a
statement than a question, and Jason looked at her as
they stopped on her doorstep.

"I wouldn't dream of living anywhere else," she
said simply. "I love it here, even in the winter. There's
nothing like watching a storm blow in, curled up in a
chair with a hot cup of tea and—"

"And a good book," he finished for her, a trace of
laughter in his voice.

Samantha looked at him searchingly, expecting to
see a mocking glint in his eyes but satisfied when she
found none. "And a good book," she echoed with a
smile. She could feel his eyes on her in the darkness,
and a small silence cropped up. "I...I had a good time
tonight," she said finally, feeling compelled to break
it. She looked away quickly, once again acutely aware
of his maleness. "I—tonight was the first time I've
ever been inside David's house. It's really very nice."

Jason didn't seem to share her unease. "Yes, it is,"
he remarked conversationally. "It's a lot like my place
in Malibu. Lots of cedar and glass, the same split-level
design." He met her eyes and smiled. "I'm surprised
you've never met David."

Samantha shrugged her slender shoulders. "I've
lived here less than a year. I suppose he's been here

during that time but we've just never run into each other." The reply was automatic, her mind on what he'd just said. Malibu. The word conjured up images of long sandy stretches of beach, expensive homes, and again—scantily clad California beauties. She almost groaned. It seemed a million miles away—as far from her reach as Jason was.

"That's something I think I'm thankful for. You're probably the only thing I've ever beat him to."

"What?" Frowning Samantha dragged her mind away from the thought.

Jason grinned. "Girls, sports, cars...you know how competitive men can be. Especially in college." He shoved his hands into his pockets and eyed her thoughtfully. "Yes, if he'd met you first you probably wouldn't be here with me tonight. He'd have snapped you up so fast you wouldn't have known what hit you."

Samantha felt her cheeks grow hot. He was talking as if she was some kind of femme fatale. She fished for her key in her pocket. "I really should be going in, Jason."

He nodded and took the key from her hand. After swinging open the front door, he slanted her a wry smile. "At least you locked it this time." When Samantha said nothing, merely looked at him, he nodded toward the doorway with his head. "I'll feel better when you're inside, Samantha."

She obligingly stepped upward, watching as he murmured a good-night and started back down the pathway.

She took a breath and called after him. "Jason."

He halted immediately and stepped back to her. She suddenly felt like a teenager on her first date. He'd made it plain the evening could have ended far differently. "Thanks again for the dinner—and the balloons," she said softly. A smile pulled at her mouth. "No one's ever sent me balloons before."

He moved forward a step. "You sure you don't want to come back and check the sheets on the bed?"

She almost laughed at the undisguised hope in his voice. From her position on the threshold, they were looking directly into each other's eyes. He was so close their faces were almost touching, her mouth only inches away from his. Her nails dug into her palms, but she quelled the impulse to lean forward and press her mouth to his.

"No." She shook her head and dropped her eyes, a rueful little smile pulling at her lips. "I'll take your word they're not red satin."

"Samantha."

She looked up quickly. "Yes?"

"I've never sent heart-shaped balloons to anyone before, either." His voice was full of laughter, but his eyes were warm and tender, and she suddenly felt her heart had taken on a pair of wings.

The glowing promise in that look was something she couldn't get out of her mind. She told herself that she was being mawkish and sentimental, that she was foolishly reading far too much into Jason's attentions. Nonetheless, her dreams were filled with visions of a laughing, dark-haired stranger. She spent that night, and the next few as well, sorely regretting her solitary bed in a way that hadn't happened since the early days of her divorce, and she woke up in the morning a very frustrated woman.

Over and over the next day she found herself wondering if that fleeting sense of magic they had felt the night before was just that—fleeting. Not for herself, but for him. Because he had felt something for her, at least she hoped and prayed that he had!

But the days passed, and she heard nothing. How many times she caught herself parting the kitchen curtains and looking out the window toward the house next door, hoping to catch a glimpse of him, she couldn't have said. For all that she knew, he could have packed himself up, lock, stock and barrel, and gone back to Los Angeles. There was absolutely no sign of him.

At the end of a week, Samantha was fuming. Much as she hated to admit it, she was convinced she'd been nothing but a playmate that night, a pleasant diversion to while away an evening. Her only consolation lay in the fact that all he'd gotten from her was a little mild petting. And what had she received in return? A dream come true... She refused to complete the thought. Pride wouldn't let her. If she'd slept with him, she'd never have forgiven herself.

Even so, there was a part of her that knew she'd never have forgotten it, either.

The thought only made her angrier. "After all," she reminded herself scathingly, "forewarned is forearmed, and you can't say he didn't warn you. A one-night stand is probably the most a woman could ever hope for from a man like him. He probably doesn't even know the meaning of the word commitment!"

Still, she was glad she was able to keep busy. She'd worked on the inside of her house during the dreary winter months, painting and papering the walls and the cupboards. The previous owners hadn't taken very good care of it. Nor had the salt air been particularly kind to the clapboard siding, but she'd had to put that off until summer. She'd spent the last couple of days scraping and meticulously sanding, taking advantage of the warm sunny weather. Today was her first day painting. It was shortly before noon, and she had finished nearly one whole side of the house.

Laying the brush carefully across the bucket of paint, she wiped her hands on a rag and stepped back to admire her handiwork. The light blue-gray she'd chosen was a vast improvement over the peeling blistered shade of yellowed white it covered.

"Not bad," she murmured approvingly, bending over to retrieve her brush. "Not bad at all—"

"Especially not from this vantage point."

The teasing voice came from behind her. There could be no question about its owner. Samantha froze. It was only when she realized the picture she presented that she slowly straightened.

She faced Jason with a glare. "I'd appreciate it if you'd keep your sexist remarks to yourself!"

"Touchy today, aren't we?" he murmured with a smile. "Would you believe it if I said I was talking about the paint job and not your—"

She cut him off abruptly. "Not in the least!" She brushed by him toward the back door, resolutely ignoring the sudden lurch of her heart at the sight of him. He was dressed in jeans and a white V-necked pullover that intensified his tan and his dark masculinity.

She scowled when she saw that he had followed her into the kitchen. "I don't remember inviting you inside," she said pointedly.

He shrugged. "What's an invitation among friends?"

"Friends? I wasn't aware that we were friends. You certainly don't seem to think so!"

Jason stared at her for a moment. "You're angry," he said in some surprise.

Samantha took a deep breath, prepared to tell him exactly what she thought of him. Even she was surprised at what came out. "Where have you been this past week?"

"Why...I've been working." He blinked at the high-pitched demand.

"Writing?"

"Yes."

"The whole time?"

"Of course."

She gazed at him for a moment, as if trying to decide whether or not to believe him. Then she turned and began to wash her hands in the sink, scrubbing furiously.

"I'd take it easy if I were you. It's only skin."

She only scrubbed the harder and darted an angry glance at him from the corner of her eye. He'd come to stand very near her, one lean hip resting against the edge of the counter.

"I didn't know if you were dead or alive." The accusing voice was directed at the sink. "For all I knew you could have drowned in your coffee cup or—or been eaten alive by your typewriter!"

She could feel his eyes on her face. "You're upset because you haven't heard from me." It was a statement, not a question.

Samantha grimaced and turned off the rush of water. He'd been working—writing. Why did it come as such a surprise that he took it so seriously? He could hardly churn out a five-hundred-page novel a year—sometimes two a year—and not work at it. She was suddenly reminded of the last year with Alan. Fresh out of college, he'd been offered a fantastic job with a firm in Portland. But the hours were long and demanding...and that was when things began to sour.

She had felt left out. And wasn't that how she was feeling now—left out?

"And you thought I might have been hurt."

She nodded, aware that it wasn't quite the truth. She took particular pains in wiping the watery trails of grayish paint from the stainless steel sink, aware of a twinge of shame at her pettiness, but it wasn't enough to erase the feeling of hurt.

"And of course there's no other reason you're upset with me."

She hated the knowing tone of his voice, as well as the note of dry humor. "No," she said shortly. Reluctantly she reached for a towel.

"I have no objection to you keeping an eye on me, Samantha. In fact, I have the perfect solution—we could move in together."

It was too much. She whirled to face him. "Oh, you know that's not it at all!" She scowled. "I'm not a nosy little busybody who spies on her neighbors. I just—I just thought that after—after that night you would have..." Her voice trailed off.

"You thought I'd forgotten about you, that you were no more than a voluptuous body and a comely face. You thought that after I'd gotten what I wanted from you—"

"Oh, stop!" She threw the towel at him. "You didn't get what you wanted, did you?" The minute the words were out she could have bitten off her tongue. It was stupid to be so upset, especially when she had no claim on him, but how she wished she did! And it hadn't been anger so much as disappointment... and he was conceited enough to know it! But she hated being so transparent. "Oh, of all the... I—I'm not voluptuous and you know it!"

There was a seemingly endless silence. Jason moved closer, so close she could see the flecks of gold in his eyes. "No, I didn't get what I wanted," he said finally. "And don't make the mistake of taking that the way it sounds." He paused, then added quietly, "And you're not voluptuous . . . you're perfect."

He knew exactly how to get to her, Samantha thought weakly. The words were precious as gold, his tone smooth as honey. And if only she could believe him. She bit her lip and turned aside. "I'm sorry," she said. "I really shouldn't have jumped down your throat. I should have known you were working . . ."

He moved to take a seat at the small maple table. "You're just not used to my working habits. I dive in and don't come up for air for days. And while I'd *much* rather be with you, I do have a deadline to meet." He stopped and she could feel his eyes on her. "But it's nice to know you care," he added softly.

"I—I didn't say that." Nervously she wiped her hands on her jeans.

Jason made no comment. Instead he turned his head to look at her. "Just because I haven't seen you didn't mean I wasn't thinking of you. In fact—" a satisfied smile spread across his features and he propped his chin on his hands to look at her "—thinking of you was very inspiring." He grinned wickedly. "Especially during the love scenes."

The love scenes. She noticed he didn't call them sex scenes this time. Her heart leaped. Did that mean . . . ? But no, she was reading too much into it. No doubt his womanizing was a reflex reaction. She sat down at the table across from him. "What's this one about?"

He raised a dark eyebrow. "I thought you'd read the last of my books."

Samantha shrugged, a little embarrassed. Despite what she'd said to him the other day, she'd picked up *Love's Sweet Bondage* just last night. But she still couldn't bring herself to read more than a few pages. She liked Jason—liked him? She was fascinated by him, but she still felt cheated in knowing he'd never emotionally thrown all of himself into his books.

She put her elbows on the table and laced her fingers together. "That doesn't mean I can't ask what this one is about, does it?"

He studied her for a moment. "I guess it doesn't," he finally conceded, then launched into an account of the book. It was the usual lusty tale, a Western-flavored romance with an added blend of intrigue and a case of mistaken identity. Samantha was well-acquainted with the theme, yet she listened intently, knowing Jason would probably have no trouble at all making this book stand head and shoulders above the rest.

"Sounds like you have another bestseller on your hands," she observed with a smile. "I'm sure it will sell especially well in Oregon, since it's set here." She paused briefly. "Do you always visit the place in which your books are set?"

"I try to. There's usually some research involved, and I think it improves the sense of atmosphere."

Samantha eyed him quizzically. "Your first book, *Desert Fires*, you went to Morocco?"

Jason laughed. "Actually that was the only one where I did strictly armchair traveling. I was writing for a television sitcom then and I just couldn't take the time—"

"A sitcom? You wrote comedy for TV?"

His lips curved up in a smile. "That surprises you, doesn't it?"

"A little," she admitted. "I could see you writing a swashbuckling Errol Flynn-type movie or something." She pushed back her chair and smiled at him a little hesitantly. "I don't suppose you'd like to stay for lunch?"

The question was asked over her shoulder as she crossed to the refrigerator. She caught his eye, but suddenly her breath rattled unevenly in her throat at the lazily seductive look in his eyes. The merest glimmer of a smile hovered on his lips as he turned in his chair to watch her.

"Is that an invitation this time?"

Samantha wanted to look away but couldn't. She was caught in the dark velvet of his voice; the faintly husky tone, which was both an invitation and a plea, had dropped by subtle degrees. "Yes," she answered softly, and suddenly felt that it wasn't an invitation to lunch she'd just issued.

His eyes moved over her, slowly, seductively, making her blood soar in a sudden rush of sensation. Never had she been more achingly aware of her femininity and how very much a man Jason was. A man in the flesh—a man she could reach out and touch...not a dream, but alive and real.

She had to tear her eyes away from him. What was it about him that made her retreat into a dreamworld, a fantasy world, a world where only the two of them existed? She looked down at her hands, laughing a little shakily, and caught sight of her worn paint-spattered jeans.

Oh, Lord, she was a mess—she had to be! Until now it had never failed to amuse her that she always managed to use twice as much paint as she really needed, half on the walls and half on herself. "Why do you always manage to catch me with egg on my face!" she muttered, half to herself, half to him. She made a mad dash for the hall. "I suppose I could go change—"

"Don't bother, you look absolutely enchanting. And it's not egg on your face, it's paint—right on the end of your nose." That velvet-edged tone was wrapped in laughter. Stricken, Samantha paused in mid-flight and encountered a pair of amused brown eyes. But suddenly his voice once again softened. "I really can't stay. Actually I came over to tell you I'm leaving later this afternoon for New York."

"New York?" Her eyes darted frantically toward the mirror perched on the living-room wall only to return in a flash to his muscled form. He had already moved to stand near the front door. New York. Her heart sank. It might as well be the moon. Her appearance was all but forgotten. She caught her breath and trailed behind him. "I always seem to catch you on the run—either coming or going. Business again?"

He nodded and stopped in the tiny entryway. "My agent called this morning. There's a movie deal in the works for *Midnight Enchantment*."

"A movie deal." She managed a shaky smile. "That's...fantastic."

Jason shrugged and smiled. "If it goes well, I should be able to wrap things up in New York after a few days. Then I'll be stopping off in L.A. to see my attorney." His last words were distinctly reluctant. A shade of disapproval lingered just under the surface. "My ex-wife is stirring up trouble again."

His ex-wife. There was barely time to assimilate the thought. Jason's eyes captured hers in a gaze so intense, so searching that Samantha felt herself slowly drawn into the dark warmth of his eyes. It was like silk sliding slowly, sensually, deliciously over every inch of her body. A sensation not unlike fire warmed her skin, quickened her breath.

"You didn't mean it, you know."

Her tongue darted out to moisten suddenly dry lips. Her whisper came haltingly. "What?"

"What you said about the two of us not being friends." There was something distinctly sensual in the honeyed warmth of his voice. "We are, you know, and I'm hoping it won't be long before it's much more than that."

Her head whirled giddily. Certainly it was what she had hoped for—that and more. But as far as it going any further...that was her own private fantasy. "Are you? That sounds almost like a promise." She meant the words to be light and flip. Instead they sounded breathy and faintly excited, exactly the way she felt, exactly the way Jason always made her feel.

"Not a promise, more like a prayer. And I give you fair warning—I'm going to do everything in my power to see that it happens."

Still caught in his spell, Samantha laughed a little shakily and tried to blithely dismiss the remark. "Spoken like a true hero."

"Spoken like a man who knows what he wants."

The quiet intensity of the words almost shocked her. Much as she longed for it to be otherwise, this verbal sparring was a game between them...or was it? She eyed him tentatively and caught a glimpse of something almost deadly serious in the back of his eyes. She hesitated, and her gaze dropped to the frankly sensual curve of his mouth to find him smiling slightly.

"Jason..." Her eyes were unknowingly wide and uncertain as they locked on his face. "After Los Angeles..." She took a deep breath and forced herself to speak. "This is goodbye then?"

His reply was adamant and instantaneous. "Not on your life." He paused and added softly, "And that *is* a promise."

As much a promise as the smoldering look he gave her before he left, a look that sent her blood pressure zipping skyward and her heart in undaunted pursuit. Her legs weren't entirely steady as she finally made her way over to the mirror, but by the time she reached it she was walking on air. A slow smile spread across her face as she eyed her reflection. The grayish-tinged paint wasn't on the end of her nose at all—it was on her cheeks, her chin, her eyebrows, even her bangs were streaked with blue-gray. She laughed out loud. She was a sorry sight. She looked like a child bent on mischief who had tumbled headfirst into a bucket of paint!

But for the first time in her life she was aware of herself, aware of her femininity, aware of her womanhood, in a way that she had never been before— even with Alan.

Jason had done this to her, she mused wonderingly. She'd been charmed, bewitched, captivated and possessed—and he hadn't laid so much as a finger on her.

Who but a fantasy man could do that to a woman? Who but a fantasy man could do that to her? She grinned rather wickedly to herself as she made her way back outside. It was like one of her favorite romances come to life—the irresistible hero tamed by a woman's love—but with one tremendous advantage.

Jason Armstrong was real—and living right next door.

Six

Samantha walked around in a haze the rest of the afternoon, amazed at the change that had taken place in herself in the space of an hour. Only that morning, she'd been burning with resentment at Jason for ignoring her. Now she was almost convinced she had him practically eating out of her hand, pining away for the sight of her.

Her mouth turned down at the corners as she got ready for bed that night. Pining away indeed! Who was she trying to kid? It should be patently obvious to even the most untried of hearts that Jason was a practiced charmer when it came to women and she was a fool if she let herself believe she was any different to him—which only brought her around to the subject of his wife.

His wife. A pang of unexpected jealousy shot through her until she remembered he was no longer

First
Class
Romance

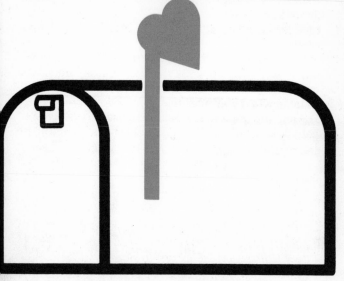

Delivered to your door by
Silhouette Desire®
(See inside for special 4 FREE book offer)

Find romance at your door with 4 FREE novels from Silhouette Desire!

Now you can have the intense romances you crave without searching for them. You can receive Silhouette Desire novels each month to read in your own home. Silhouette Desire novels are modern love stories for readers who want to experience firsthand *all* the joyous and thrilling emotions of women who fall in love with a passion that knows no bounds. You can share in the passion and joy of their love, every month, when you subscribe to Silhouette Desire.

By filling out and mailing the attached postage-paid order card, you'll receive FREE 4 new Silhouette Desire romances (a $9.00 value) plus a FREE Mystery Gift. You'll also receive an extra bonus: our monthly Silhouette Books Newsletter.

Approximately every 4 weeks, we'll send you 6 more Silhouette Desire novels to examine FREE for 15 days, *before they're available in stores.* If you decide to keep them, you'll pay just $1.95 each (a savings of 30¢ off each book) with no charge for home delivery and at no risk! You'll also have the option of cancelling at any time. Just drop us a note. Your first 4 books and Mystery Gift are yours to keep in any case.

Silhouette ❦ Desire®

A FREE
Mystery Gift
awaits you, too!

Mail this card today for your
4 FREE BOOKS
(a $9.00 value) and a Mystery Gift FREE!

Silhouette ❤ Desire®

Silhouette Books, 120 Brighton Rd., P.O. Box 5084, Clifton, NJ 07015-9956

☐ **YES!** Please send me my four SILHOUETTE DESIRE romances, *free*, along with my *free Mystery Gift!* Then, send me six new SILHOUETTE DESIRE books every month, before they're available in stores, and bill me just $1.95 per book (30¢ less than retail), with no extra charges for shipping and handling. If I am not completely satisfied, I may return a shipment and cancel at any time. *The free books and Mystery Gift are mine to keep!*

NAME _____
(please print)

ADDRESS _____

CITY _____ STATE _____ ZIP _____

Terms and prices subject to change.
Your enrollment is subject to acceptance by Silhouette Books.

CAD825

married. And he hadn't exactly sounded thrilled when he'd mentioned his wife—not at all. A tiny feeling of self-satisfaction pierced her sudden ill-humor but died just as swiftly. The elusive Jason Armstrong, as elusive as the man behind Cathryn James. He'd wasted no time in making sure she knew it—and still knew it, for that matter. The man whose heart would remain forever unchained. The man no woman could capture no matter how tempting her wiles.

But some women had captured him. And she couldn't help but think it very likely that he had decided marriage was too confining, that he had discovered he could never attain a lifetime's happiness with one woman. Still, she couldn't stop herself from wondering about his ex-wife.

Samantha's mind continued to wander once she was snuggled beneath the blanket, thinking of Jason in New York. Many of his books had lush exotic locations—India, Spain, the Caribbean...so many places. And he'd been to all of them. He said his home was in Los Angeles, yet she wondered how much time he actually spent there. Didn't he ever feel the need to settle in one place?

The thought was jarring. Her father had never wanted to. She rolled over in bed and propped her hands behind her head, staring at the eerie shadows dancing on the ceiling. She could hear the gentle motion of the ocean undulating against the shore, but the sound, usually so soothing, had no effect on her unsettled emotions. She and Jason were so...so different. They were on opposite ends of the earth when it came to the subject of love. Jason obviously thought nothing of jetting across the world, while to Samantha there was nothing more welcome in the world than coming home, whether from a hectic day dealing with her second-graders, or from a quick trip to Astoria to see her mother.

A faint feeling of unease crept into her heart. Jason had promised he would be back, but considering the way he flitted around the world she wouldn't hold her breath. Her father had made promises, too—some he'd broken, some he hadn't. He had shown her that promises were something easily given, not so easily kept.

On that cautious note, Samantha finally turned over and slept.

She spent the next few days finishing up the paint job on her house, somehow half expecting Jason to sneak up behind her with some outrageous teasing remark and that devastating grin. Impatient with herself for letting him dominate her thoughts to such an extent, she finally decided to call her mother early Wednesday morning.

"Samantha! I was going to call you tonight! How are you, dear?"

Somehow her mother's bright chirpy voice was slightly irritating. Samantha lifted a hand to her forehead and massaged her aching temples. Damn! Why was she so edgy? Because Jason was gone, a niggling voice insisted.

She pushed aside the thought. "Fine, mom," she answered absently. "I thought I'd come visit for a few days. Feel like company this weekend?"

"You know better than to ask! I've been expecting you for several weeks already!"

"I—I've just been tying up some loose ends around here." And trying to corral Jason Armstrong? The thought vaulted into her mind without warning.

"What time can I expect you, Samantha? Will you be stopping in Seaside to see your friend?"

"My friend?" Samantha drew a complete blank.

"Your friend in Seaside—your roommate in college."

Her friend the sex fiend. The memory overtook her as she recalled the morning Jason had surprised her stepping from the shower, and a heady feeling of warmth suffused her body despite the fact that she was alone. She took a deep breath. "I've decided not to after all. I'll probably leave early in the afternoon but I'll stop by the shop as soon as I get in."

As it was, Samantha debated telling her mother about Jason as she loaded her suitcase into the back seat of her dark blue Volkswagen on Friday. She and her mother had a very close relationship, they'd had to, since all they'd had was each other for so many years. But what could she say? "Mom, I've met the most fantastic man. He's all I ever wanted..."

She could almost hear her mother's cheerful hopeful tone. "Sounds serious, Samantha. Is it?"

And then what would she say? "It could be, if I let it. At least for me—but never for him. You see, he doesn't believe in love." No, the subject of Jason was better left untouched.

She had a very pleasant visit with her mother and some old friends, stayed five days, and came home on Wednesday. But the slight upswing in her mood didn't last more than a few minutes after she pulled into the driveway. She couldn't help but notice that Jason's silver BMW was conspicuously absent from the driveway next door. A thick layer of sand covered the small block of asphalt, crunching under her sandals as she stepped out. The surf was roiling and vicious-looking as it washed up on the sand, the foam-flecked waves matching the leaden-gray color of the sky. Overhead was a thick layer of clouds, churning and twisting as they forged their way north.

A fierce gust of wind blew her hair across her face as she searched her purse for the key. She was still combing her fingers through it to restore a little order when she set her suitcase down in the living room and walked toward the kitchen.

She stopped short on the threshold. She was never sure why, but her eyes were drawn upward to the plaster ceiling. "Oh, no!" she groaned. What she saw made her heart sink. Several large splotches marred the surface of the plaster. Dammit, her roof was leaking! It had rained lightly in Astoria the night before and that morning, but there must have been a downpour here. Her mouth drooping, she changed into jeans and an old plaid shirt, heaved a ladder from the garage and clambered onto the roof.

She was cautiously optimistic about what she found. A number of faded black shingles in an area above the kitchen were either damaged or completely blown off, but she was hopeful that the entire roof wouldn't need to be replaced—at least not right now. A few more years and she wouldn't mind, but her little car was also showing signs of wear and tear. She couldn't pay for a new roof if she couldn't make it to her job, and a new car would probably have to take priority over a new roof.

Mindful of the blustery wind, she made her way slowly down the sloping incline toward the ladder. She was nearly there when a fierce gust of wind snatched at the lightweight aluminum ladder. It toppled over in front of her horrified eyes and crashed to the ground.

"Lord, what next?" she moaned aloud. She crept to the edge and looked down. The house was old, higher than many of its low-slung contemporaries. It was maybe fourteen feet to the ground. Her eyes shifted toward the beach. It was deserted, except for a few people several hundred yards away—too far for them to hear a plea for help.

The wind tore at her hair and shirt, its chill penetrating the thin cloth. She shivered. At times, late June on the Oregon coast wasn't much warmer than any other month of the year. Samantha looked down again, an odd feeling in the pit of her stomach. She had no choice but to jump. The sidewalk edged the house, and she doubted she could clear it and make a cushioned landing on the grass.

"Oh, well," she murmured in meager consolation, "at least if I break a leg I'll have the rest of the summer to recuperate."

She flexed her knees and cautiously raised herself. It was then that she saw Jason emerge from the sliding glass doors of the house next door onto the deck. He was back!

"Jason!" She swallowed her excitement and stood up a little further. "Jason!"

He remained where he was, looking out to sea, strong hands braced on the cedar railing. Samantha called to him repeatedly, but the sound was carried away by the wind. Finally she stood up as far as she dared and waved her arms, praying that in this precarious position on the edge of the steep roof she wouldn't suffer the same fate as her ladder. *"Jason!"*

Finally his head turned. She made a sweeping gesture with an arm, repeating it until he had stepped off the deck and started toward her. She was too far away to see the expression on his face but it wasn't hard to imagine the amazement that must have been written there at the sight of her perched on the roof.

At last he stood on the ground below, grinning up at her. "What on earth are you doing up there?" He shook his head and perched his hands on lean denim-covered hips. "Don't tell me—it's just as I thought. The woman with her feet planted firmly on the ground with her head in the clouds is trying to get a little closer to the stars? Or chasing rainbows instead?"

Samantha scowled. She should have known. Why was it that this man and this man alone had a knack for finding her in such ridiculous situations?

"The wind blew my ladder over! Just put it back up against the house and then you can leave!" she snapped. "I can find my own way down!"

"Not on your life!" Before she knew it he'd swung the ladder up against the house and was scrambling up the rungs. His dark head poked over the eaves. "A lady in distress! This is my big chance to be a real hero—probably my only chance! Even you wouldn't be so cruel as to take it away from me!" He grinned at her and crooked a finger at her. "As soon as you swing your feet over the side, all you have to do is put your arms around my neck and leave the rest to me!"

Samantha's jaw dropped. "You—you can't mean to carry me down!" she sputtered. "Why do you have to play at being a hero *now!* Weren't you ever a boy scout?"

"Never had the honor," he said smartly.

She glared at him. "You idiot! You'll break your back—you'll break *both* our backs!"

His eyes made a leisurely appraisal of her body, which was crouched before him. She felt a tingling sensation in her breasts despite the dancing lights in his eyes. "You're not all that heavy, are you?"

Samantha rolled her eyes skyward. "Will you please move so I can get down?"

"Not a chance," he repeated stubbornly. "I could just as well go home and pretend I never saw you—and take the ladder along with me." His eyes began to dance again as he added hopefully, "Unless you'd rather I caught you when you jumped?"

With that Samantha gave in. She lowered one leg cautiously over the side of the house and inched her way onto the ladder next to Jason. The only way the two of them could fit between the narrow metal rails was to face each other and she found that to keep her balance she did, indeed, have to curve an arm around Jason's neck. She'd been cold only seconds before, but now her skin burned where his hand rested on the small of her back. It seemed to take an eternity to reach the bottom. By that time her breathing was shallow and irregular—and it certainly wasn't from fear.

Their bodies were fused together from the neck down, her curves molded intimately against his lean contours. Her face was mere centimeters away from his. Their noses brushed several times as he cast a downward glance every so often to guide their descent. Samantha found her eyes lingering on those firm lips so close to her own. To her horror, she found herself wondering if he was as affected as she was by the unavoidable movement of their bodies against each other. She uttered a silent prayer that he was!

Jason didn't speak until they had reached the bottom. "How about an instant replay?"

His other arm had come around to encircle her, bringing her even closer to the taut length of his body. His breath was warm against her face, his tone very husky.

A gentle finger lifted her chin. "I missed you, Samantha. I missed you . . . very much."

Every fiber in her warned against him—he was a charmer, a sorcerer, a rake. But at this moment, Samantha wanted nothing more than to be charmed. He was looking directly into her eyes, and what she saw in his made her heart leap wildly. Was there a woman on earth who could help but respond to such a man? Certainly this one couldn't. Excitement skittered along her spine and the way she quivered all over, she wasn't sure she would be able to stand if he let her go.

"I—I missed you, too," she said softly, and knew with every ounce of her being that she didn't lie.

"You're very agreeable all of a sudden." His tone had lightened, but the look in his eyes hadn't. "Will this mood continue...through the night?"

Something inside her responded to the elemental blaze in his eyes. "For the next few minutes at least," she whispered.

"Do I dare press my luck?" He bent his head so that his mouth rested just at the corner of hers.

Her fingers slowly explored the muscled contours of his shoulders, covered by a layer of beige cambric. It took a tremendous effort to talk, even to breathe. "Maybe...you should."

"Maybe I will."

The soft tone touched something inside her even as his mouth brushed slowly, evocatively, across hers. His hands moved down ever so slightly to lightly grasp her hips and pull her to him. Her pulse jumped erratically at the intimate contact but she reveled in the supple feel of his flesh beneath her fingertips and the taut strength of his thighs molded against her own. She gasped when his lips claimed hers more fully, his tongue demanding entrance even as she gave it.

When Jason finally released her mouth, he looked down at her, his eyes on her trembling lips. "We don't have to worry about your nearest neighbor watching," he said softly, "but there's a better place for this."

Samantha's head was spinning and she hardly realized when he tugged on her hand and led her inside. It wasn't until his body propelled her gently backward on her bed that she understood what was happening. She made a small murmur of protest.

The tiny sound was swallowed by his mouth over hers. Samantha was achingly aware of the hard length of his body as it lay over hers, of the subtle distinctions between their bodies. Her breasts were crushed by the unyielding bulk of his chest, her legs tangled in the sinewy length of his. He kissed her again, a kiss so warm and tender and so full of promises that she shook with the delicious feelings it roused in her. Her heart seemed to stand still.

"Jason—" Her voice shook with the effort it took to speak. Was this right or wrong? She'd entered into a relationship willy-nilly once before, expecting the sun, the moon and the stars. Would she regret it if she and Jason made love? Or would she regret it more if they didn't? Heaven help her, she didn't know! She could scarcely think!

"Jason, please... I—I can't do this."

"Sure you can." His voice was warm and faintly teasing against the corner of her lips. "All you have to do is relax while I do all the work. But the next time..."

Samantha closed her eyes against the picture his words evoked. For a moment all she could see was her naked limbs entwined seductively with his, his dark face smiling brilliantly up into hers.

"Jason, please! I'm sorry, but I can't!" Her voice finally rose above a whisper. "I—I have to think about tomorrow!"

"I don't care about tomorrow." The hoarsely muttered words were muffled against the upward slope of one breast. Half the buttons of her shirt were already undone.

His head was dark against the pale skin already revealed, the contrast so deeply inviting that her hands expressed an alarming tendency of their own to bury themselves in his hair as his lips continued their torturous magic over her skin. It was only by clutching fiercely at his shoulders that she stopped herself.

"But I do!" She took a deep shuddering breath. "I wish I didn't but I do!"

His body stilled against hers. One lean hand moved upward to trace the curve of her jaw, the touch almost unbearably tender as he lifted his head slightly to gaze up at her. "You can't say no," he murmured softly. "You don't want to say no."

That was beside the point. Couldn't he see that? A summer affair was all he could possibly want from her, perhaps not even that. A fling. Could she settle for that? Deep in her heart she knew she couldn't. Not from Jason—not from any man. If they made love she would expect all that should rightfully come with it— emotional ties, commitment. All that was dear to her heart Jason blithely brushed aside. She wanted love, and he wanted sex.

The thought scared her as much as it startled her. Her heart began to thump with thick uneven strokes.

She pushed frantically against his chest even as her fingers tangled themselves in the silky mat of hair revealed by the opening of his shirt. "I—I can't say yes, either!" she moaned.

And somehow that seemed to say it all. She felt his eyes boring into her, and never in her life had she felt so miserable. His fingers covered hers and guided them over his chest so she could feel the rapid rhythm beneath.

"Be still, my heart," he murmured softly.

There was something almost mocking in that velvet tone, and Samantha looked quickly away. Silently he pulled away from her and tucked his arms under his head, looking at the ceiling. She sat up slowly on the edge of the bed.

"I should have asked you to come to New York with me," he remarked conversationally. "Wooed you, courted you, wined and dined you.... You'd have liked that, wouldn't you?" He paused. "Could I have won you over, Samantha?"

Her fingers trembled as she struggled to fasten her shirt. If he had done all those things, would they have meant anything? Or would they have been no more than empty meaningless gestures, a means to an end. "Why didn't you?" she asked, and then wished she hadn't.

"Would you have come?" he countered quietly.

Again, she felt his eyes on her. They no longer touched, but she was as much aware of his body sprawled next to her on the bed as if they were wrapped in the most intimate of embraces. "I—I don't know," she whispered miserably.

The words seemed to hang between them, creating an invisible barrier. "You see now why I didn't ask. I didn't have time to let you weigh all the pros and cons before deciding." His tone was light, almost bantering, but there was no denying the slight mockery and impatience.

It wasn't lost on her. "Did you really expect me to just leave everything at the drop of a hat and go away with you?" she said stiffly.

He shrugged his shoulders. "Why not?" That dark brown gaze sent a prickly feeling up her spine as he gave her a long probing look. "There's nothing wrong in indulging yourself once in a while—accepting a dare, taking a chance. There's an element of chance in everything we do, especially in love." He laughed softly, and Samantha had the feeling he was baiting her. "But you haven't discovered that yet, have you?" he asked softly.

Her eyes narrowed as she turned to look at him.

"We make our own destiny, Samantha. You can't sit on the sidelines forever and expect opportunity to come knocking on your door. You're just not a gambling woman, are you?" He sat up as her back stiffened. "You're almost a female Jekyll and Hyde—prim and proper on the outside, while inside there's a hopeless romantic who wants nothing more than a white knight to sweep her off her feet. But if that actually happened you'd probably be afraid to go along for the ride."

She bridled at the amusement in his tone. He was probably only needling her because she refused to go to bed with him! "You make it sound like I'm a shrinking violet!" she muttered.

"Oh, I wouldn't go quite that far. Your tongue is a little too tart for that." He flashed what would have been a disarming grin under any other circumstances, then his look grew thoughtful. "But it doesn't hurt for someone to let themselves go once in a while—you included."

Samantha glared at him. "You really think I'm prim and proper?" she demanded.

"Without a doubt," he informed her brashly.

"And naturally if it was up to you, you'd prefer that I was fast and loose!" she retorted hotly.

"Oh, never that," he vowed promptly, but the gleam in his eyes belied his words.

Samantha watched as he stretched out again on the bed. He looked very big and relaxed lying there, but above all, so intensely masculine it nearly took her breath away. Suddenly she knew what he was doing— he was waiting for her to make the first move, handing control over to her. It was there in his eyes, warmly inviting but faintly challenging. He wanted her to be the aggressor and take charge of whatever might happen. And how she wanted to! It was crazy, absolutely ridiculous, for her to say he made her mouth water, but that was how she felt.

Only the knowledge that he wouldn't let her retain control for long stopped her. There was too much of the male hunter in him for that. And if things ever progressed too far, would she be able to stop him? Would she want to stop herself?

She glanced over her shoulder at him. "You only want me because you can't have me," she muttered.

The minute the words were out of her mouth she knew they were a mistake. They were much too provoking to a man like Jason—to any man, she recognized belatedly.

He was across the bed like a flash of lightning. "Who says I can't?"

He was quick but she was quicker. She bounced off the bed and was across the room as his hands grabbed empty air. "Jason, stop," she pleaded, half laughing, half in earnest. "How did this conversation ever get started!" she moaned.

"It started because you refused to go to New York with me."

"You never asked!"

"But you would have said no and we both know it!"

Samantha sighed. She wouldn't admit any such thing, because he was the one who might have been surprised. He had the power to turn her life completely upside down, and she had the feeling he knew it! "You wouldn't have wanted me tagging along anyway," she protested halfheartedly, "especially if you were going to see your wife—"

"My *ex*-wife—and the matter was between our attorneys. As it was, I didn't have to make the trip to L.A. after all. The business took care of itself." He looked at her rather oddly. "Is that what's bothering you? My ex-wife?"

Samantha shook her head, a little confused by the emotions rioting through her. "I don't know." She hesitated. "Well...maybe. I'll admit I've wondered what kind of woman could make you fall in love with her." She drew an unsteady breath. "Was she pretty?"

"Yes." Jason seemed to hesitate. "More than that—she was beautiful."

An unexpected pain squeezed her heart. So his wife was beautiful. She hadn't wanted to hear that, and yet even if Jason had denied it she would have known. "Were you...married long?"

Again he seemed to hesitate. He rose and moved to stand at the window, watching the waves crash against the jagged outcropping of rock on the shoreline. "My marriage took place during the hot-blooded days of my youth," he responded lightly. "A time when even the best of us are given to excesses. How long was I married to the beautiful Hollywood starlet?" He smiled thinly. "Too long, it seems. Now if you don't mind, I'd much rather talk about something else."

She was only too glad to dismiss the subject. She wished now she hadn't bothered to ask about his wife. Taking advantage of her place near the door, she left the intense atmosphere of the bedroom behind. Jason followed her into the kitchen where she forced her mind elsewhere.

She gestured up at the stained ceiling tiles. "I don't suppose you know anything about roofing?"

She made the remark simply to break the uneasy silence between them, but she gaped as he began to roll up his shirt sleeves. "As a matter of fact, I do," he said calmly.

"You?" She blinked disbelievingly, then had to tear her eyes away from the sight of those muscular forearms.

"I worked my way through college, and I was brought up not to be afraid of a little hard work." He studied her for a minute. "Or don't you trust me to do a good enough job?"

She would trust him with just about anything, she suddenly realized—except her love. Somehow it made her warm toward him, while at the same time knowing it was best to keep a safe distance away. There was, she suddenly realized, a lot to admire about him. And it wasn't only his looks, she assured herself hastily. Yes, there was more to Jason Armstrong than brawny biceps and a good-looking face. He was diligent, hardworking, intelligent, and he'd made a niche for himself in the romance publishing world. Probably not an easy task, especially since a man would undoubtedly have two strikes against him from the start.

Impulsively she laid a hand on his arm. "Of course I do," she told him, smiling a little shyly. Her eyes met his, and the sudden flare of warmth she saw there made her senses swim. She had to turn away or lose herself in those toasty brown depths. "I think there are some shingles in the garage. I hope they're not too old to use."

"They're fine," he assured her once he had examined the string-bound bundle. One knee bent on the concrete floor, he looked up at her suddenly. "I don't come cheap, you know."

Samantha blinked. "Cheap?" she echoed.

"Not much comes free these days—the best is never free."

"The best!" She gasped indignantly. Why, of all the conceited, egotistical... "Maybe I should hire a roofer from Lincoln City," she informed him icily. "Or better yet, I could do it myself and probably do just as good a job as you!"

"So you're as resourceful as you are pretty." His grin was back in place. "An irresistible combination in a woman—now I know why I'm falling so hard." He shifted to both feet, picking up the bundle of shingles as he rose. "Is supplying the food for a picnic on Sunday asking too much in exchange for repairs by an expert roofer?"

An expert roofer... Falling so hard... Who was he trying to kid? He was no more an expert roofer than she was, and she was the one who had been falling since day one, and he probably knew it!

She shook her head. "Jason, I don't think—"

"That's the trouble with you—you do a little too much thinking." He paused to grab a hammer from the assortment of tools hanging from the pegboard on the wall, then looked back at her over one broad shoulder. The warm intimate look in his eyes sent her pulse racing madly. "Two o'clock okay?"

"Two o'clock is fine." She wasn't even aware that she had spoken until he was halfway to the house. She stood and stared as he scrambled up the ladder as if he was a monkey. He had done it again, she thought in amazement. Seduced her with his eyes—and with his words! If she had any brains she would tell him what to do with his picnic! If she had any brains she would forget she had ever set eyes on Jason Armstrong!

If she had any brains she would take this chance at heaven in whatever way, shape or form she could, and worry later about the consequences.

Much later that night she voted strongly in favor of the latter.

Seven

But Samantha later reflected that Jason was right—she could never be totally free and fanciful and carefree. There was too much to be lost, and everything to gain. Life with her father, and Alan, had taught her that much at least. She'd never had a casual fling with anyone. To her, body and soul were only to be given and shared if the relationship was serious. Alan, in fact, had been her first and only lover. Could she handle an affair with Jason, with each of them going their separate ways when the summer was over? But maybe it wouldn't come to that, she later told herself cautiously.

And then again, maybe it would.

It was a question she wasn't sure she wanted to answer. For the first time in her life, Samantha found herself procrastinating. She didn't want to think about tomorrow, or next week, or even next year.

Instead she thought of how much she had now, at this moment. She had never thought it possible that she could grow so close to a man who couldn't share her beliefs in what was perhaps the most important thing in life—love. But it was happening, and it was wonderful. Samantha knew he was taking precious time away from his grueling writing schedule, yet it seemed to bother her more than it did Jason.

They had dinner together nearly every night—at his place, at hers, at a quiet restaurant in Lincoln City. They walked on the beach on moonlit starry nights. They laughed and talked about silly things, mundane matters, everything but affairs of the heart. The one thing that was on Samantha's mind more and more, and the one thing she wanted to avoid at all costs.

Jason gave her his undivided attention, made her feel beautiful, young and utterly feminine as she'd never felt before. But even while she basked in the warmth of those feelings, she knew she couldn't let herself fall for him as she longed to do. So she urged herself to tread lightly, as lightly as he.

But she was never quite sure if she was succeeding.

Sunday dawned clear and beautiful. Hazy streamers of sunlight floated down from the sky, gilding the dancing waves of the ocean with a bright dazzle. At precisely two o'clock, Samantha and Jason walked along the beachfront not far from home. Sheltered on one side by an outcropping of rock and by a pile of driftwood on the other, the tiny alcove protected them from the wind and prying eyes alike. They spread a blanket on the warm sand, and while Samantha unpacked the hamper she'd brought along, Jason unrolled a fluffy beach towel he'd tucked under his arm, grinning when he brought out a bottle hidden in the folds.

Her eyes widened. "Champagne!" she exclaimed, then looked at the food spread on the blanket. "With fried chicken and potato salad?" She laughed and pulled one last item from the hamper. "I brought paper cups!"

"That's all right." The cork flew open and he reached for one of the cups. "Drinking champagne from paper cups doesn't make the occasion any less special."

Samantha broke off a chunk of crusty French bread and handed him a plate. "What's the occasion?"

"I finished the first draft of *Quest for Love* last night." His eyes grew warmer by degrees as they met hers across the small blanket. "But that takes second place to the real occasion. Any time is special when I'm with you."

Her heart turned over at the smile he gave her but she forced her attention to his first words. "You're finished already?" she asked in surprise. "You've only been here a few weeks."

"It was in the works before I came." His eyes took in her slim figure, clad in a white one-piece terry sun-suit. Tied loosely at each shoulder, it showed off the light honey tan of her bare legs and arms. "And I did say once I was feeling especially inspired—thanks to you."

Despite his avid gaze, a feeling of dread suddenly gripped her. "So now that it's finished you'll be sending it off to your publisher?" Her heart fluttered as she nibbled on a chicken leg. That wasn't the real question and she knew it. It somehow brought home the fact that there was an end in sight for the two of them, an end she wasn't yet ready for.

His low chuckle surprised her. "It's a draft, Samantha. I usually do at least two—change a few things here and there." He shrugged. "Maybe add a scene or cut a few." He paused for a moment before adding quietly, "That reminds me, have you finished *Love's Sweet Bondage* yet?"

Her eyes flew to his face. He was studying her openly, his look intent. It was a shock to realize he actually looked almost grave. Her gaze faltered a little under his scrutiny. The merest hint of a smile now played at his lips, but that indefinable emotion in his eyes seemed to have deepened. She sensed that it was somehow important to him that she finish the book— but why? Confused, she looked away.

"No guts, Samantha? Can't you tell me to my face that you've found a replacement for me already?"

Her head whipped around immediately. The familiar ring of laughter was back in his voice. Oddly enough, she'd grown used to grappling with it, and it was easier to deal with than the side of him she had just glimpsed. "It didn't bother me when we first met," she shot back. "Why should it now?"

The grooves near his mouth deepened. "Why indeed?"

With that the ball was dropped in her lap. "No," she admitted grudgingly. "I haven't found a replacement for you yet, and I haven't finished the book, either." She wasn't about to admit it to him, but it wasn't for lack of trying. She'd read half a dozen romances over the past few weeks, and while they were good, they weren't fantastic, as all of his were. Or had been. She was a little angry at having to remind herself.

"Poor baby." His look was tenderly indulgent as he grinned. "Would it make you feel better if I told you this is the last book on my contract and I'm thinking of doing a thriller?"

"Infinitely!" She wrinkled her nose at him. All her exasperation fizzled out the second he flashed that entrancing white-toothed grin. "Here—eat this!" She passed him a small bowl filled with plump ripe strawberries. "There's nothing like fresh Oregon strawberries, and since I can't seem to keep you quiet maybe they can!"

Strangely enough, they seemed to do the trick. Not very many minutes later, Jason stretched out on the blanket beside her. He reached for the hand that rested on her upraised knee. "You're not still mad at me, are you?" he murmured, and pressed a warm kiss on her palm.

His head was very near one slender thigh, and as he turned it toward her, the sun's rays slanted down on his dark head. Samantha fought the impulse to tangle her hands in those dark lustrous strands. "I wasn't really mad to begin with," she answered softly. Her skin still tingled all the way up her arm from the brief contact of his mouth on her hand.

Moments later, his deep even breathing told her he was asleep. Samantha got up and stretched her limbs, looking out at the lacy patterns the surf made on the sand. The distant chatter of children laughing and playing drifted to her ears. Feeling utterly serene and content, she lay down next to Jason and soon joined him in slumber.

The sun's rays burning on her eyelids woke her an hour later. She opened her eyes, and looked straight into Jason's face. She had somehow moved closer to him in her sleep, and one strong arm was curved around her waist. He had turned onto his stomach, with his head toward her. Not wanting to move for fear of waking him, she studied the dark features so close to her own—the tiny laugh lines extending from the corner of his eyes, the thick bushy brows, the straight blade of his nose.

She smiled when her eyes lingered on his mouth. It was full and sensuous, and she ached to trace the firm masculine shape with her fingers and run them along his roughly textured jawline.

His eyes opened then and looked full into hers. "Good morning," he said softly.

A slight smile curved her lips. "It's afternoon, silly." Still caught up in the pleasure she derived from looking at him, she let her eyes slide down his body when he turned on his side to face her.

"You're staring at me," he said after a moment.

Reluctantly she looked up at his face. "Am I?" she murmured. Her eyes moved down his body again, and a wicked glint appeared in his eyes.

She felt her cheeks pinken as he grinned, but she couldn't prevent her eyes from moving down his body yet again. He was clad in a light-blue T-shirt and skimpy pair of darker-blue nylon shorts that left little to the imagination. The taut muscular thighs and lean flanks were clearly defined, as was the part of him that made the two of them so different. Just thinking about his male essence caused an insistent heat to sweep along her veins, and she became acutely aware that breathing space alone separated their bodies.

"I don't mind if you look, Samantha." He grinned and added in a stage whisper, "I'll even let you touch."

And touch she did, drawn to him by a force more powerful than anything she had ever felt before. He still lay on his side, and Samantha's slim hand crept tentatively to his waistline before sliding down over his abdomen. Her fingers slid beneath his T-shirt, raking lightly through the dense mat of hair that covered his chest and abdomen.

His hand caught hers on its second downward journey. "On second thought, I'm not sure I should let you take such liberties with my person." The words were light, and he was still smiling, but there was a flare of passion in his eyes that hadn't been there before.

Pleased, Samantha smiled and left her hand where it was, tangled in the wiry curls near his navel. "You have a funny way of talking sometimes," she said softly. "Just like in your novels."

"I know," he said dryly, then smiled. "Too much...bookwork."

A couple walked by just then, and suddenly reminded of their surroundings, she withdrew her hand and sat up. Beside her, Jason bounded to his feet and drew her up with both hands.

"Let's build a sandcastle," he said with a grin.

"A sandcastle!" The afternoon sun was glaring, and she squinted up at him. "You—and me?"

"You and me. As in us." He laughed at her doubtful tone. "I can't believe you've lived on this beach for a year and never made a sandcastle! The woman with stars in her eyes and all those outdated romantic notions about—"

"Don't say it!" Her eyes gleamed a warning. "Don't you dare make fun of me, Jason Armstrong!"

"Make fun of you?" Even with his eyes full of laughter he managed to look wounded. "Not a chance," he vowed fiercely. Then with a chuckle, he grabbed her around the waist and lifted her completely off the ground, twirling her around and around in his arms until she was dizzy.

Feeling suddenly buoyant and free, Samantha pushed at his chest until he lowered her to the sand. "Enough!" she laughed. "You win—we'll build a sandcastle!"

They moved toward a stretch of beach where the sand wasn't as dry and loosely packed. The next few minutes found them down on their knees in the sand, carefully scooping up sand for the shell of their castle.

"Hey, Miss Monroe!" The high-pitched exclamation came from a youngster who nearly fell while scrambling up to Samantha. "Guess what? The girl next door had to have her independix out!"

Jason looked at her. "Her *what?*" he mouthed silently.

Samantha smiled. "She had to have her appendix out?" she asked the little boy, stressing the word slightly so he would hear the difference. He seemed so proud, she couldn't bear to correct him. "My, that's such a big word for you to remember!"

Kevin beamed at her praise, then did a double take at their excavation. "You buildin' a sand castle, Miss Monroe?"

Her eyes met Jason's warm gaze and she nodded to the little boy.

"Gee, I wish I could help." His eager voice encompassed both her and Jason, but he looked to Jason for an answer. "Do you think I could, Mr. Monroe?"

Jason looked up at him. "Of course," he assured him gravely. "Miss Monroe and I—" here he looked at Samantha, his eyes twinkling "—could use an expert pair of hands."

As it was, they were soon joined by a group of half a dozen children, several of whom had been in Samantha's class the previous year. With the help of the youngsters, the castle slowly took shape. Jason offered encouragement while Samantha showed several small pairs of hands how to firmly mold the sand into the desired shape.

An hour later, the two adults and surrounding youngsters stood back to admire their work. A large moat filled with sparkling seawater, diligently hauled bucket by bucket by several of the children, surrounded a castle complete with ramparts and battlements, a gatehouse and a tower at each corner.

"I thought you didn't know how to build a sandcastle," Jason commented dryly. "You were the one telling the rest of us what to do." He cocked an eyebrow at her. "Medieval history major in college?"

"Elementary education," she informed him loftily, "with a minor in psychology."

He shook his head. "I guess I don't have to ask about your source then, but I know it wasn't one of my books."

Samantha wrinkled her nose at him. "It wasn't," she told him lightly. "It was about a Scottish earl who kidnap—"

"I know the story well," he proclaimed melodramatically. "A fierce and black-visaged warrior kidnapped the beautiful and hot-tempered daughter of his most treacherous enemy and imprisoned her in his castle—a tale of fiery lust and tempestuous passions unleashed by the fury of love..."

"Oh, you!" Samantha ended up laughing along with him, but her eyes grew dreamy as she gazed at the sandcastle.

"Daydreaming again, aren't you?" Now that the castle was completed, the children scampered off in all directions. Jason drew her back with him to their sheltered section of beach.

Samantha smiled but said nothing. He pulled her down on the blanket and dropped down beside her. "Let me guess." One lean finger turned her face to his and he stared into her eyes. "You're pretending you're a fairy princess who might have lived in such a castle, wishing for the day a noble knight whose chivalrous deeds were known throughout the kingdom would come and claim her as his bride, the woman of his dreams."

She couldn't help but giggle. "And you think you're the noble knight, I suppose."

He spread his hands wide. "Why not? After all," he added, his eyes gleaming, "I did rescue you from your roof."

Samantha groaned. "You also managed to smoke us out of your house, and your intentions were far from honorable in either case!"

"My intentions were no different than any man with half a brain and a normal set of hormones." His eyes moved lingeringly over her slender figure with a thoroughness that left her breathless.

Before she knew it, he moved so that his body was in front of hers, trapping her between his outspread hands. Samantha was forced to lie back on her elbows, half reclining on the blanket. His eyes dropped to her mouth. "But you are the woman of my dreams," he said softly.

A murmur of protest formed on her lips, but the words died in her throat. They were so close she could see the hazel flecks in his eyes. She felt confused, unsure of him. She'd never been wholly comfortable with his free and easy compliments, and couldn't help but wonder why he persisted. Were the words second nature by now, a reflex action of the romance writer who was a master at his craft? Or did they come from the man himself, straight from the heart? Something inside her yearned to believe him, and yet she knew instinctively that she was probably a far cry from many of the women he had been involved with, including his ex-wife. What was really behind his attraction to her—if indeed there was one?

Yet why would he bother with her when he could probably have any woman in the world he wanted?

"Jason..." Her hand came up to rest on his muscled chest, not resisting, but not inviting, either. "I—I love the way you talk sometimes, and—"

"And the way I make you feel." The words were self-assured yet, strangely enough, far from arrogant as he looked down at her, his weight supported by his hands.

"And—and that, too. But I wish you wouldn't say things you don't really mean."

"Things I don't mean!" Both dark eyebrows slashed upward. "What makes you think I don't mean them?"

"Jason, you make a living juggling words around on paper. And maybe—maybe once you found out I was a tried-and-true romance lover you thought I'd get a kick out of hearing what every woman secretly dreams of." She hesitated. "And I did..I mean I *do*...but I also know you're telling me what you think I want to hear. What I mean is...how many men tell a woman they've known only a matter of weeks that she's the woman of his dreams!"

"I do." There was no trace of laughter in his face as his eyes bored into hers.

Samantha's breath caught at the fierce blaze in his eyes, a blaze that only made her quiveringly aware of the lean strength of the body so close to her own. Jason did not touch her anywhere, yet she couldn't have been more aware of the heat and hardness of him had they been wrapped in an embrace only lovers assume. Why did he have to be so utterly irresistible? She fought to keep hold of her thoughts as she tried to ease away from him.

"Me and how many other women?" she refuted desperately.

"None."

The note of gravity in his voice stunned her. She felt herself weaken. Gullible, that's what she was. But she actually wanted to believe him. "Do you honestly expect me to believe that?" she argued weakly. "Not even your wife?" She swallowed as Jason stiffened. "I mean your ex-wife?"

She wasn't prepared when he sat up abruptly. His forearms rested on his knees as he stared out to sea. "Why should I?" He laughed, a short bitter sound that held no mirth. "She had plenty of other men around to tell her."

She stared at him, not sure what to make of his reaction. His face hardened, a face that was foreign to her and seemed totally alien to his nature. What was he thinking? Painful memories perhaps? Despite the warmth of the sun's shimmering rays beating down on her shoulders, she shivered. The profile so coolly presented to her seemed cold, almost hard. He seemed a different man from the teasing easygoing charmer she'd come to know—and love?

A painful ache closed her throat, making the words difficult. "You—you must have loved her very much."

"Love was the last thing she wanted, or needed, from me." He almost spat the words. He seemed on the verge of saying more, but then his mouth clamped shut and his jaw tightened. "Look, can we please—"

"I know," she interrupted as lightly as she could. "We went through this just the other day, remember?" Her eyes seemed to burn as she glanced over at him. "End of subject. Closed, period." She attempted a laugh, but it ended up a soft sigh instead. "Now, am I a perceptive person or not?" Aware of Jason's eyes on her, she rose and began to repack the hamper. Her movements were mechanical, her mind a million miles away from what she was doing. All this time she'd thought Jason didn't believe in love—*her* kind of love—but he must have been in love with his wife for him to react like this. The subject was a volatile one, that much was clear. The most painful ones usually were, she realized sadly. She knew from experience. She'd spent many a sleepless night pondering what had gone wrong with her marriage, and it had taken a long time to admit that she and Alan had never been right for each other in the first place. He was sweet and kind, but he'd never really been aware of her needs and her wants.

But she was convinced Jason's anger was only a mask. Maybe he had never wanted the divorce to begin with. Maybe he was secretly hoping that someday he and his ex-wife could get back together. Maybe... She closed her eyes against the thought. The possibilities were endless and she didn't want to think of them.

"Samantha." He reached out and touched her arm as she bent to shake the sand out of the blanket. "Don't take this the wrong way."

She forced a smile but gently shook off his touch. "I'm not," she said, folding the blanket.

"You are. I can see it in your eyes." This time his fingers curled around her wrist in a grip that wouldn't be denied. The blanket dropped to the ground as he pulled her back down beside him. They faced each other on the sand, knees bent and nearly touching. "My ex-wife doesn't mean a thing to me, Samantha," he said fiercely. "Even in the beginning—"

"You don't have to explain, Jason." Her eyes grew troubled as she looked up at him. He looked regretful, grim and oddly determined. He opened his mouth but one of her hands reached up to cover it. She hesitated, not sure how to explain. If Jason had chosen to confide in her about the whys and wherefores of his divorce when they had first met, she might have felt differently. Even when she'd found out about his beautiful wife, she hadn't wanted to think about her. She hadn't let herself think about her. But as it stood right now, what she didn't know wouldn't hurt her any more than she was hurting right now.

"Samantha." His hand reached up to cover hers where it still lay against his mouth. He pressed a scalding kiss to her palm before dropping it to his side, her fingers twined tightly in his. "I'll admit I don't like talking about Natalie, but it's not for the reason you think."

"Jason," she said, gently withdrawing her hand and gathering all her courage, "I'm not...the sort of woman you're usually attracted to, am I?"

She glanced up to find a look of surprise on his face. "Exactly what kind of woman do you think that is?" he asked in a moment.

"Oh, I don't know." She failed miserably in matching his bantering tone. "The usual blond Hollywood bombshell or long-legged dark-haired vixen." She could have cheerfully buried her head in the sand when the words came out sounding strangely like a wail. Indeed her gaze dropped, and she traced idle patterns in the sand—a square, a circle, a tiny heart.

"I'm well acquainted with the type, yes. All glitter and dazzle and not the slightest bit of warmth." Despite the teasing tone, she suspected there was more than a grain of truth in the words. "All shallow and empty-headed—" his voice dropped suddenly, playing across her skin like the elusive brush of a feather "—and all in the past." He lowered his voice even further. "Actually, I think it's time I looked for a woman to stimulate my intellect . . . and now that I've found her, there's only one woman in my future from now on. Believe me, Samantha, glamour and glitz doesn't have a thing on you."

Samantha nearly groaned. Swinging away from him, she drew her knees up and watched a pair of gulls struggle against a current of wind. "Jason, please!" She pushed her hair back away from her face. "I'm serious. I'm not sophisticated or worldly but I wasn't born yesterday. I don't fit the mold and we both know it! Why are you even bothering with me?"

The words seemed to surprise Jason as much as they did her. She glanced over and caught the tentative expression on his face. But when he laughed, she could have cried.

"Do you have to ask?" A warm hand touched the curve of her cheek and turned her face to him. "After an honest forthright statement like that, do you really need to ask?" His smile deepened. "But you're right, you're not like anyone I've ever known before." His eyes touched on every facet of her features, his eyes so warm and soft she felt her heart lurch in her chest.

His hand cupped her chin gently. "Do you know how it feels to come outside after a spring rain and find the sun shining brightly? It's like looking at the world after a gauzy veil has been lifted, seeing everything through a fresh set of eyes. Everything is bright and golden, glistening in the sun, and the air is sweet and pure. That's the first thing I noticed about you, Samantha. You're fresh and unspoiled, almost as innocent as those children who helped us build the sandcastle. It's like—like you haven't learned yet how harsh life can sometimes be."

But she had. She had known pain when her father walked out on her and never came back. And later, when she'd finally recognized that she and Alan could never make it together, she had known hurt and despair, even a sense of failure. But she listened intently, his husky voice blending with the almost mesmerizing warmth of his eyes.

"It's been a long time since I've known anyone like you," he finished softly, looking deeply into her eyes. "Far too long."

Something inside her seemed to flower and grow. The slanting golden rays of the sun touched his head. His hair shone with dark luster, and she ached with the need to smooth the wind-ruffled strands that fell on his forehead. Her hand lifted to one broad shoulder and swayed toward him, her eyes soft and luminous. "Jason..."

But whatever she might have said was never spoken. The quiet moment of intimacy was broken when a bright yellow Frisbee whizzed by, narrowly missing their heads. Jason pulled his hand away from her face and sighed, casting a disgruntled eye toward a pair of teenage boys. A reluctant smile tipped his mouth as he got to his feet and extended a hand to her. "How would you like to go for a drive?"

Samantha nodded. Even if she'd wanted to refuse, she couldn't have said so. For in that moment when their eyes had met so intently, the most amazing thought had come crashing into her mind. She'd told herself over and over this past week that a woman would have to be crazy to fall in love with a man like Jason.

And she was definitely feeling a little bit crazy.

The giddy feeling lasted while they picked their way up the narrow trail that led from the beach. They decided to drop off the hamper and blanket at Samantha's before leaving.

"Whose car are we taking?" she asked.

"Not your little Volkswagen," Jason commented dryly. "I don't care to have my knees wrapped around my shoulders for the rest of my life."

"Oh, come on," she protested as they crossed the patio. "It's not that bad, at least not in the front seat."

His eyes took on a sudden gleam. "Come to think of it, the back seat doesn't sound so bad after all, except I think we're getting a little old for that kind of thing."

His words inspired a vivid picture in her mind of entwined limbs that sent her pulse racing. "Maybe we should take your car instead," she muttered.

A low chuckle sounded behind her as Jason opened the front door for her. "Sounding better and better all the time," he murmured as she brushed by him.

Samantha laughed shakily but made no comment. She looked back over her shoulder as he stopped near the entryway, an odd look on his face. "What is it?" she asked.

He looked down at the doorknob. "Funny," he said. "I could have sworn I saw you lock that door."

"I thought I did, too." With a shrug she went on into the dining room and put the hamper on the table. She was about to turn back to him when a blurring motion caught her eye.

"Samantha! How are you, sweetheart?"

The next thing she knew a warm pair of arms enfolded her in a snug hug and an equally warm kiss was pressed on her mouth. When her head cleared she found Alan's delighted face swimming in front of her eyes.

Something akin to shock washed through her. Jason stiffened behind her, and she could sense his cold disapproval. The feeling went through her like a razor-sharp rapier, while Alan's laughing blue eyes danced before her. She froze, wishing she could disappear into the earth below, but she was caught between the two men like a mouse in a trap.

Alan finally looked over her shoulder at Jason, a smile creasing his face. In his typical friendly manner, he brushed by Samantha's still figure and thrust a hand into Jason's, pumping it vigorously.

"Alan Monroe here," he greeted Jason enthusiastically. "And you are...?"

Samantha's eyes flitted to Jason's stern face, her only movement so far. Never in her life had she seen anyone who looked so coldly forbidding. He didn't even bother to speak to Alan. Instead his icy gaze fixed itself on her. "Alan Monroe," he repeated in a cutting tone. His eyes seemed to rake over her. "Your—brother?"

Alan finally seemed to have noticed Jason's cold reception. "Uh...not exactly." He retreated a step before the taller man to stand at Samantha's side, casting her an uncomfortably quizzical look.

Samantha swallowed. Alan was leaving it up to her, as he rightly should. Oh, but to be a coward and run with her tail between her legs!

Unfortunately, that wasn't one of her choices.

She made a vague gesture between the two men. "Alan, this is Jason Armstrong. Jason, this is Alan—" she cleared her throat "—my ex-husband."

Eight

The silence that followed was like a bomb blast. "Your ex-husand," Jason finally repeated. "Somehow I don't seem to recall you ever telling me you were once married." His voice was chillingly polite as his gaze traveled from Alan to Samantha and back again. "Do you mind telling me how you got in here?" he finally asked Alan pointedly.

Samantha shivered at the contempt in his eyes. She'd never seen Jason angry before, and from the harsh expression on his face, she didn't think she'd ever want to see it happen again. He looked very big and powerful, and yes, even rather dangerous, as he leaned against the door frame of her dining room.

Alan broke the uncomfortable silence. "Since Sam wasn't here, I knew she wouldn't mind if I let myself in," he said with an uneasy glance at Jason. "I used the key she gave me when I stayed here last spring."

Samantha's heart sank to her feet. Of all the things for Alan to say!

He seemed to have realized it, too. He attempted a grin, ending up with a sickly looking smile at best. "Sam wasn't here of course."

"Of course," Jason echoed coldly. He crossed his arms over his muscular chest and looked directly at the shorter man. "I hope you weren't planning on spending the night, because three in a bed can be rather crowded." A forced grin twisted his lips as his eyes ran leeringly over Samantha's figure. "And I can guarantee Samantha is going to have her hands full."

Samantha gasped at the blatant implication. Poor Alan didn't seem to know what to make of it. "Ah, Sam...I was just on my way to Coos Bay and I thought I'd stop and see how you were...but I can see you're fine." He backed toward the front door, running a shaky hand through his sandy curls. "Maybe now is as good a time as any to return this—" He fumbled in his pocket and thrust a key into her palm, then turned and practically ran from the house. A moment later the roar of a car engine could be heard.

Samantha's fingers clutched the cold metal of the key. She felt like flinging it into Jason's face. His audacious speech infuriated her, and she drew herself up proudly. "You had no right to do that," she said clearly, her eyes a vivid shade of blue in her pale face. "No right to be so rude! No right to *insinuate* that we...that we..." Her face reddened, and she stumbled over the words.

"That we're sleeping together?" he finished for her. Amusement flared in his eyes for an instant, before a harsh glitter replaced it once more. "Why shouldn't I?" he asked moodily. "It's going to happen sooner or later. You've led me on a merry chase for long enough, and I think it's time it ended."

The belligerence in his tone was at complete odds with the strange light in his eyes as they ran boldly over her slim figure, lingering on the heaving motion of her breasts beneath the thin material.

Samantha's heart beat thunderously in her chest, but solely from anger, she told herself. She was angry with Jason, furious that he'd had the nerve to let Alan believe they were lovers. But somehow the woman inside her couldn't help but respond to that wholly masculine look.

She backed away from him, her hands gripping the back of a chair for support. "You think you're irresistible, don't you?" she flung at him. Her pulse pounded furiously as he straightened from the doorway and shortened the distance between them. "That all you have to do is crook your little finger, just like all the heroes in your books, and every woman within a hundred-mile radius will be at your beck and call..." The words were choked off as he came closer yet.

Her knees went weak as he rounded the chair and gripped her bare shoulders. "Why are you fighting it, Samantha?" His voice was heart-meltingly tender, a soothing caress on the frazzled ends of her temper. "You want me as much as I want you. Why can't you admit it?"

His eyes dropped to where her breath was coming in short hard bursts. Her own closed briefly—the mere touch of his hands had done that! She didn't want to be forced into something she wasn't sure she was ready for.

"Don't," she whispered unsteadily. "I can't...we want different things, Jason." An exquisite sensation spiraled through her as his hands traced delicious circles on her upper arms, her shoulders, wherever they touched. His mouth brushed hers, the caress maddeningly elusive as she was lifted and deposited gently on the sofa. His hard body pressed hers into the cushions. Her hands curled into fists at his shoulders as she fought the urge to slide her hands into the thick blackness of his hair. She moaned softly. "Jason, please . . . I can't . . . I just can't."

She was totally unprepared for the effect her words had on him. That warmly tormenting mouth ceased its restless exploration of her face and neck. Jason raised his head to look at her, and suddenly there was a tempest raging in his eyes.

"You mean you won't," he said harshly. He pulled away from her and stood up abruptly. "Is it Alex? Are you still in love with him? Is that the real reason he still has a key to your house?" He laughed bitterly. "You couldn't live together but you can still love together?"

Samantha jumped up, now as furious as he. "His name is Alan," she reminded him icily. "And this has nothing to do with him. In fact, I completely forgot about him having a key!" She glared at him. "He's a salesman for a pharmaceutical firm in Portland but sometimes he has business in other parts of the state. He had to make some contacts in this area last spring so I let him spend a few nights here. It was during spring vacation and *I* was spending the week with my mother in Astoria! Now are you satisfied?"

"Why didn't you ever tell me you'd been married?"

That was a very good question indeed. She averted her eyes and sat down abruptly. "You never asked," she muttered.

Jason's mouth tightened. "What an answer," he said disgustedly. "You could have told me, you know. You *should* have!" he accused in the same tone. "You knew what was happening between us—"

"What was happening between us!" It was her turn to glare at him accusingly. "I know you've been trying to weasel your way into my bed from the start! And *you* knew from the start I could never settle for just sex and you made it very plain that was all you were about to offer! Now tell me—tell me chapter and verse—why I should have told you about my ex-husband when you've stated *several* times that you didn't want to talk about *your* ex-wife!" She sniffed indignantly. "I'm supposed to confess all while you get to sit back and just listen? That's not the way it works, Jason Armstrong!"

Bingo—she'd scored a direct hit. She could see it in the mottled flush that crept beneath his tanned cheekbones. "Are you saying that if I'd told you more about my ex-wife you'd have told me about Ale— Alan?" he asked roughly.

Samantha blinked—another very good question. Why hadn't she told him about Alan? She looked away from that demanding stare. "I might have," she muttered, "if I thought there was ever a chance of anything serious developing between us."

"And of course you think that's impossible."

She hated the mockery in his tone. She knew the score, she'd be a fool if she pretended otherwise. "I do," she defended staunchly. "You'll be leaving soon, a matter of weeks." There—her choice was made. So why did she feel so rotten?

"And you're convinced your body is all I want from you." The look he gave her seemed to reach into her soul. "Two lonely people, drawn together in the night..."

What was he trying to do—beat her into the ground? But there was no mockery, no teasing, no laughter in his voice. She was lonely, though it wasn't something she admitted often. It was easier, so much easier to pretend.

She drew a shaky breath. "What! Don't tell me you're lonely, too!" The laugh she gave was forced. "Forgive me if I have a difficult time believing you have a problem finding a woman to share your bed at night! After all, look what you've got going for you— looks, money..."

The flippant voice trailed off. And what about her? She'd had a chance at marriage and happiness once, and she'd failed miserably. But what she said was true. Jason did have everything. No doubt he had droves of women falling at his feet back in Los Angeles.

She might have felt a spurt of triumph at the uncomfortable look that flashed across his face if it hadn't hurt so much. As it was, she felt as if a giant hand was squeezing her heart.

She sensed rather than saw him move toward her. "You know what the hell of this is?" he said roughly. "I actually believe that your ex-husband having a key to your house is really what you say it is. And it's crazy, but all of a sudden I'm wondering why you don't love him. Was it because he didn't live up to your expectations of what a husband should be—of what you thought love should be?" His voice hardened as he looked at her. "Your kind of love is white knights and fairy tales, and maybe that's why your marriage failed. Maybe you couldn't pull your head down from the clouds long enough to get a glimpse of reality. Hell, you still can't for that matter! You really believe all that drivel—that love is perfect, that love is forever, that love conquers all.''

Samantha pressed hot hands to her cheeks, his words whirling around in her brain. His words were like a whiplash to her heart. "I have to," she said shakily, "or I'll end up like you. And I'd rather be a dreamer than a cynic.''

"And are you any better off than I am?" His voice was harsh, accusing. "Do your dreams fill the void in your heart or satisfy your longing to be held by someone during a cold winter night? I want you and I'm not afraid to admit it. *You* want a storybook hero, a fantasy man, the kind of hero that's only found in those blasted books you read. But the truth is you're a coward, Samantha. Even if such a man existed you'd be afraid to try to find one in the flesh. At least I'm not afraid to go after what I want—what I need.'' The hard look in his eyes sent splinters of pain slicing through her. "There's something missing in your life, Samantha. When are you going to own up to it?''

For an instant she almost hated Jason, hated his ability to reach into her mind and pluck out her most private thoughts. Alan had been her first and only lover. And somehow, at this moment, tense though it was, she was more conscious than ever of what she'd lost since her divorce—the sharing of feelings, the sense of security that belonging to another and being one with that person had given her. Perhaps most of all, she realized how much she missed the physical side of marriage. But she couldn't—and wouldn't—satisfy the craving of her body and sacrifice her emotional well-being in the bargain. She had every right in the world to expect the two to go hand in hand. She clung to the thought the way a drowning man might hold on to a life preserver. It had happened once, no matter that it had been all too fleeting, and it could happen again. But deep in her heart she knew she harbored a secret fear that was almost as great as her need—the fear of dealing with failure once more.

She was afraid to love again, but just as afraid not to love.

The seconds ticked by slowly. Her pain was a throbbing ache in her breast. He knew—damn him, he knew! She felt naked and exposed in a way that had never happened before, even in the days following her divorce. But suddenly she realized something else, as well. Jason said she wanted a hero, the kind of hero that was only found in romances. But wasn't that how she'd thought of him all along?

Yes, she'd found her hero. She was in love with Jason Armstrong, a man who carelessly tossed aside and belittled all that she held dear to her heart.

The realization brought a wave of pain so intense she nearly cried out. She pressed her fingers to her temples, confusion roiling in her brain. She couldn't stand here anymore and listen to him tear her apart little by little with his cutting words. The atmosphere was stifling; she couldn't breathe. She started for the door, but in the second before she reached it, her wild eyes met Jason's, and she couldn't hide the agony in her heart. And then she was running out the door, running blindly down the path to the beach, darting past a party of picnickers, weaving through a group of children.

She didn't recognize the startled look in Jason's eyes, or see the hand thrust after her. She didn't hear the hoarsely muttered sound that was her name as he stared after her.

Samantha ran until she thought her lungs would burst from lack of air, but she welcomed the pain. It took her mind off the ache in her heart. Her breast heaved from the unaccustomed exertion when she collapsed on the sand, unable to go even a step farther.

She sifted through a handful of sand, letting the rough grains trickle through her fingers. She'd kicked off her sandals somewhere, and the sand felt cool against her bare feet as the sun lowered in the late-afternoon sky. A chill breeze whipped through her hair. She shivered a little but lifted her face and let the wind lay bare her seething emotions, welcoming the unexpectedly calming effect.

She loved Jason. Hot tears scalded her eyelids for an instant, clouding her vision as she gazed out at the silver-glazed expanse of ocean. It was crazy—impossible. He was wrong for her, and even if he wasn't, he would soon be gone. He'd said he wanted her, but could she accept him at face value? Could she accept him as he was and ask no more? She exhaled sharply only to catch her breath in remembered anguish, experiencing once again the sharp prick of his words.

So many questions, so few answers. But one thing was certain—she hadn't run from Jason so much as she'd been running from herself.

With a sigh she picked herself up and plodded back toward home, the water occasionally lapping at her feet. She was nearing the beach in front of her house when she saw Jason, standing at the edge of the sand, looking at her. Waiting. Watching. The distant chatter of children was all but drowned out by the sudden pounding she heard in her ears as she stopped where she was.

And then a strange thing happened. She was too far away to see the expression on his face, but she could sense the twisted jumble of emotions inside him as surely as she felt her own. With an aching sensitivity, she knew she wasn't the only one hurting inside.

Her eyes locked with his as she began to move forward.

"Miss Monroe! Hey, Miss Monroe!"

Samantha glanced to the right and waved distractedly at Kevin, but suddenly she stopped short. Kevin was perched high above her on the jutting pile of rocks that stood sentinel on the beachfront.

"Oh, my God," she breathed, her heart leaping to her throat. A wave of pure panic swept through her. She lifted both arms and frantically waved them to the little boy. "Kevin, get down here! For God's sake, come back down!"

But even as she yelled to him, a frothy lick of surf nipped at her ankles and her voice was lost in the wind. Kevin merely waved and clambered farther upward. The tide was coming in at an alarming pace, Samantha realized. Within minutes, Kevin would be stranded on the rocky bluff. The waves that dashed against the lonely island at high tide could be vicious on a windy day, easily capable of sweeping away a youngster, and the wind blew more fiercely by the second.

Samantha wasn't even aware of moving. She plunged through the thigh-deep pool of water at the rocky base. Heedless of the cutting edges of the rock against her bare feet, she scrambled steadily upward until she reached the little boy.

He turned in surprise as she gathered his small body into her arms. "Kevin!" She hugged him, nearly squeezing the breath from him. "You shouldn't have climbed up this far. The tide is coming in!"

His blue eyes were wide as saucers as he peered at the churning waters below them. His voice quavered as he looked back up at her. "How—how are we going to get down?"

Samantha didn't answer until she had led him around to the beach side of the rocky ledge. Settling herself against the narrow surface, she pulled him down into her lap. "We'll be okay," she said with a surety she was far from feeling. Icy water sprayed over them and she knew with a sinking feeling the worst was yet to come.

Kevin's teeth chattered. "C-couldn't we c-climb back down and s-swim back to the beach? It's not that f-far."

She cradled him more tightly and shook her head. "The water would be too deep by the time we got back down." If she had been alone, she might have tried it, but as it was . . . it wasn't so much the water's depth as the treacherous undercurrents. Kevin's slight weight would be carried away too easily, and even if she tried to make it across with him in tow, he could lose his grip. She shivered as she glanced down at the swirling eddy below. No, she couldn't take the chance.

"We'll be all right," she tried to reassure him. She pointed to the crowd that had begun to gather at the receding shoreline, then smoothed his dampened blond curls. "Someone will come soon."

The next sheet of water was like a blow as it pounded their figures, a dense curtain of moisture. They were both drenched to the skin in the space of a second. Samantha shivered and wrapped her arms around Kevin more tightly, trying to infuse some of her warmth into him.

How long they huddled together against the bite of the wind and the chill of salt spray, Samantha could never have said. It seemed like hours before a dull roaring sounded in her ears, a drone that grew steadily louder. She opened her eyes as she realized what it was—the throbbing sound of rotors.

"Kevin!" She shook the still form lying limply against her. "Look!" She pointed upward to where a makeshift chair was already being lowered.

His eyes widened as she lifted him to his feet. "Wow! A Coast Guard helicopter! Wait 'til the kids at school hear about this! This'll knock 'em dead!"

Samantha laughed shakily at his little-boy glee. He might not have missed this for the world but this was one experience she could have done without.

A short time later Kevin's mother gave him a sound scolding then proceeded to clasp him tightly in her ample arms. Samantha was next. She acknowledged the woman's gushing thanks and warm hugs with a weak smile. Clutching the rough woolen blanket someone had draped over her shoulders, she disengaged herself from the surrounding crush of bodies.

"Samantha!" Hard hands caught her firmly by the arms before she found herself engulfed in a warm pair of arms, snugly folded against a warm male body. "Whatever possessed you to do something so stupid, so foolhardy, so completely idiotic! Didn't you think before you went charging up there?"

The harsh sound of Jason's voice was at complete odds with the tender brush of his lips on her forehead, her eyes, her cold cheeks. She sagged against his hard strength. "You told me once I did too much thinking," she murmured with a weak laugh against his chest.

His hands pushed her back so he could stare down at her. "My God!" he said fiercely. "When I think what could have happened! You could have been swept out to sea ... drowned!''

The agonized frenzy in his voice wasn't lost on Samantha. Numbly she raised her head to stare back into his hard face, the worry lines etched into his forehead, the deep grooves carved beside his mouth. But his eyes ... She caught her breath. She was dead-tired, her entire body felt like an ice cube, but the emotion reflected in his eyes had a startling effect on her. He looked protective, fiercely so, and distinctly possessive, but perhaps strongest of all ... Suddenly she felt as if a warm ray of sunshine had penetrated her foggy state clear through to her soul. In anyone else she'd have sworn it was love.

Her breathing grew shallow. Did this mean there was hope for him yet?

Jason took one look at her pale face and gathered her up in his arms. Feeling as if she'd just come home after a very long journey, Samantha wrapped her arms around his neck and drowsily smiled her contentment against the strong brown column of his neck, taking a deep breath of his heady male scent.

"Take me home, Jason," she murmured tiredly against his jaw. "Take me home."

A warm bath, some hot soup and an hour later, Samantha felt completely revived. So much so, in fact, that Jason's solicitous behavior was getting a little annoying. She slapped away his hand as he reached to take her pulse for the third time in the past ten minutes.

"For heaven's sakes, Jason," she protested, "I'm perfectly fine!" She glared at him.

"You were soaked to the skin. Haven't you ever heard of hypothermia? Maybe we should still take you to the hospital."

Samantha rolled her eyes and set aside her teacup. Jason had taken her to his house, and now they were sitting on the edge of the bed, where he'd brought her a tray immediately after her bath.

"You said yourself we weren't out there more than fifteen minutes. That's not long enough to develop hypothermia. The paramedics said both Kevin and I were fine. Isn't that enough for you?"

"You only stopped shivering a few minutes ago," Jason said accusingly. His eyes darkened and he reached out to fold her in his arms. "Samantha, I nearly went out of my mind! I don't know which was worse—seeing you up there and knowing there wasn't a damn thing I could do or having you run out on me."

He broke off abruptly, and she had the distinct sensation that he was having a hard time garnering his emotions. She couldn't help but remember the deeply intense look in his eyes when he'd brought her here. She snuggled closer and tucked her head under his chin, smiling her contentment.

"Samantha—" He expelled a harsh sigh, his breath stirring her hair. "I'm sorry. God, I'm sorry!" The words were wrenched from deep inside him. "I shouldn't have struck out at you the way I did, but I was angry, and hurt that you hadn't cared enough to tell me you'd been married."

She made a small murmur of protest and tried to look up, but his hand smoothed her hair and held her tightly. "No, don't talk, just listen," he said in an emotion-rough voice that was all the more precious for the gentleness of his hand on her head. "I don't think

I'll ever forgive myself for tearing into you like that. I know I'll never forget that wounded look in your eyes. I don't want to hurt you like that again—ever. I accused you of being a coward, but I was wrong. I'm the one who's a coward. I came after you, but when I saw you sitting there on the sand . . .''

His arms tightened as he hesitated. "For the first time in my life, I was at a loss for words. Saying I was sorry just didn't seem enough, and all of a sudden I was scared to death that you would never forgive me, that you would hate me forever for hurting you so.''

Forever. It was a strange word coming from a man who didn't believe in forever. She could hardly believe what she was hearing. Slowly she raised her head to look at him, her eyes searching his face. "Jason . . .'' Her throat tightened with emotion.

"I'm going to make you a promise, Samantha," he said in a velvet-soft tone. "I walked away from you then, but I'll never walk away again." Her skin tingled when he slowly brought her hand to his lips, brushing his warm mouth over her knuckles. There was a silent question in his eyes as they met hers.

"I'm a very forgiving woman." She smiled mistily up at him. "And I think you already know I was coming back to you when I saw Kevin up on those rocks.''

Jason's eyes grew stormy. "I still can't believe you did that!''

"I knew he'd never get down alone." Her tone was very gentle, and the lines in his face seemed to relax. His hand reached for hers, his long fingers threading tightly through hers and resting on her bare thigh.

"I know," he said with a sigh. "I'd have done the same thing myself.''

At this she smiled and drew back from the circle of his arms. "Your big chance at a real rescue attempt," she teased, "and this time it wasn't one of your make-believe heroes that beat you to it, it was the Coast Guard. Disappointed?"

His eyes met hers, the look undeniably warm. Samantha was suddenly reminded of how he had impersonally stripped her and lowered her into the tub, and just as matter-of-factly toweled her hair and body. But now his warm protective attitude was suddenly transformed into something very different, and infinitely more exciting.

"Not yet." He shook his dark head, a ghost of a smile at his lips. "All of my books invariably have a scene like this." His eyes dropped to the pale blue material that covered her slender body. "Even down to what you're wearing—one of my shirts. And we both know what happens next—a love scene."

A love scene. Her senses already whirled giddily from his nearness, but she noticed dazedly that once again, he didn't call it a sex scene.

"You know you're driving me crazy."

The sound of his voice drifted across her skin like a kiss of a warm summer breeze. She drew a deep quivering breath. "Why...is that?"

"Because after sitting here next to you, and holding you in my arms, all I can think about is the fact that you don't have a damn thing on under that shirt."

Her breath quickened. "My clothes aren't dry yet," she murmured needlessly.

"They won't be dry until morning," he said quietly, his eyes on the outline of her breasts. His eyes came up to linger on her face. "You're beautiful, Samantha."

She felt her nipples tighten and swell under the heat of his look. "I'm not," she said with a breathless laugh. "You dried me so thoroughly I'm sure I'm still red as a lobster!"

"Your nose *is* sunburned again—" his smile deepened slightly "—but you look absolutely adorable."

Adorable! How could he tell her she was beautiful one second, and adorable the next? Children were adorable; warm cuddly puppies were adorable. She shook her head and laughed shakily. "What is this fixation you have with my nose?"

That deep intimate glow in his eyes grew more intense. "It's not just your nose," he murmured in a voice that was faintly teasing, "it's your entire body—everything about you."

She stifled a groan. If only she knew when to take him seriously! "Jason—" She opened her mouth to protest.

He interpreted her look with pinpoint accuracy and raised an eyebrow. "I've just bared my soul to you and now you're going to give me that nonsense about not believing a word I say."

"Jason, please stop!" His name was half-laugh, half-groan. "I—I know I'm not pretty—my hair is a mousy brown, I have a pug nose..."

"When are you going to learn!" His fingers pressed urgently into her shoulders. "There's every bit as much to love outside as there is inside." He shifted his position on the edge of the bed and moved so close his hair-roughened thigh brushed the smoothness of her own.

Samantha shrugged uneasily. "I still have a hard time believing you'd want a woman for her mind..." She broke off, again feeling miserable.

His laughter startled her, as did the golden sparkle in his eyes. She drew herself up indignantly, but he reached for her, easily quelling her squirming movements by tightening his arms around her. The laughter in his eyes died as suddenly as it had erupted.

"You have everything," he told her in a voice like melted honey. "You *are* everything—all I've ever wanted." His voice dropped to a mere whisper. "I've been waiting all my life for a woman like you, Samantha. And now that I've found you I'll never let you go."

She was stunned by the vibrant urgency in his voice. Her eyes sought his as if seeking confirmation, unable to believe what she was hearing.

"Did you know that you have tiny threads of gold in your hair? They shimmer in the sunlight, and in the firelight." His voice rippled over her skin like wine-dark velvet. He smiled as he touched the silky strands that lay on her shoulder. "And those beautiful blue eyes, with those gold-tipped lashes. When you smile it's like a thousand tiny stars light up in your eyes. And that mouth—" his eyes dropped, and his smile faded "—I can't look at you without remembering how sweet you taste, and thirsting for that warm honey—" A finger crept inside her parted lips to trace the sensitive flesh just inside her lower lip. "Right here." His eyes looked directly into hers. "You *are* beautiful, Samantha."

She felt the sensual magic of his words, the fiery glow in his eyes, everything about him, vibrate through every part of her, clear to her soul. No man but Jason had ever told her she was beautiful. No man but Jason had ever endeavored to appeal to the deeply romantic passion in her heart. And she wanted to believe. Even more, she wanted to believe that Jason believed. A quiet serenity spread through her as she smiled at him. Never before had she felt so proud, so incredibly alive, and yes, even beautiful. Jason might someday belong to another and he might belong to no one.

But right now he was hers. And that was all that mattered.

Nine

For a long moment Jason simply stared down at her
cradling her close. "There'll be no nighttime enter
tainment in the form of a book for you tonight, Sa
mantha." His tone was incredibly soft, his look
tenderly possessive. "Tonight you're mine. All mine."

The words reverberated through her, bringing a
welter of excitement in their wake. Samantha matched
the unshakable resolve in his eyes with a look of he
own. "Does this mean I'm finally going to have my
way with you?" she murmured. Her hands slipped
over the straining muscles of his shoulders.

Jason laughed huskily. "Do with me what you
will," he quoted softly. And with that, he reversed
their positions so that she was free to do exactly that

His body looked very big and dark on the light gol
of the bedspread. He had removed his shirt, and Sa
mantha's breath stopped in her throat at the sight o

the muscled contours of his chest. A strange curling sensation formed deep in her belly as she looked at him. He was still watching her, a half-smile on his lips, but there was something in those glowing dark eyes that told her exactly how serious he was.

It was an invitation no woman in her right mind would refuse. Her hand reached out to tangle in the silky jungle on his chest, and she leaned forward to touch his lips with her own, gently at first, and then with increasing urgency.

They were both breathing hard when she finally lifted her head. His heart beat a pulsing rhythm beneath her questing fingers. One silky thigh was tangled between his, the contact of his hair-roughened skin against her own smoothness incredibly sensuous.

She smiled against his hard mouth. "So this is what's known as unbridled lust," she murmured.

His hands tangled in her hair to bring her mouth to his. "All-consuming mists of passion?" he suggested throatily.

Samantha arched her body sinuously against his. A blazing fire leaped in his eyes, exciting her further. His hands moved impatiently to the buttons of her shirt. "Insatiable desire," she countered provocatively. It was wonderful to be able to taunt and tease Jason like this. Her eyes darkened suddenly as his shirt was pulled from her shoulders. She felt the heat of his gaze burn through her as his eyes moved irresistibly to the gentle mounds of her breasts. It was even more wonderful to be making love with him like this.

His hands moved to gently cup her rounded flesh. He shook his head as her eyes linked with his. "Something far more complicated—" he muttered as he trapped her mouth beneath his "—and much more meaningful."

Somehow the words never managed to penetrate as his fingers moved to trace lingering circles over her breasts. She felt the brush of his fingers on her bare skin, the tips faintly rough but incredibly arousing. Her breath caught in her throat as she found her eyes drawn to the sight of his dark hands against the gleaming paleness of her rounded softness, coming ever closer to the budding pink rosebuds. Her eyes remained glued to his as he rose and removed the last remaining barrier between them, throwing his filmy shorts aside impatiently.

The last muted rays of the sun shimmered through the open window, bathing the proud male physique in all its glory a gleaming shade of bronze. Samantha felt the insistent heat inside her burst into flames at the sight of him.

"Jason..." Her voice trembled. The husky entreaty sounded strangely like a moan as it passed from her lips. Even she couldn't be sure if it was a plea for him to continue this maddening seduction of her senses or a protest to stop before she threw away every principle she had ever believed in. But nothing seemed to matter, nothing except the feel of his hands on her body when he joined her on the bed once again.

Her fingers crept across his chest, raking through the curly mat of hair to explore his skin, warm and faintly damp. The male scent of him swirled around her, a scent more powerful than any aphrodisiac.

"Hush, sweet...just let me love you."

That low voice was incredibly tender, the sound intensifying the fiery mist of passion that surrounded her. Her fingers clung to his shoulders as his tongue swirled around one taut nipple and then the other, bringing her to a fever pitch. It was like nothing she had ever known before, this tight aching curl of pure sensation inside her.

"God, Samantha!" His mouth was buried at the base of her throat as his hands stroked a flaming line to catch her hips in his hands. His fingers curled into the softness of her flesh. He raised his head, his eyes blazing fiercely in his face and showing more clearly than words the strain he was under as he held himself back in order to prolong her pleasure.

"Jason," she moaned softly, and a melting feeling swept through her body as he took her mouth hungrily. His tongue crept into her mouth and began an evocative exploration even as his lean hips undulated against hers in a corresponding rhythm. She gasped at the feel of his vital male force probing between her softness. Now...Jason...*now!*

The melding of their bodies was as explosive as she had known it would be, yet it was something else entirely that touched a chord deep in her soul. Their eyes were linked together by a force beyond control. Jason shuddered, his eyes drifting slowly closed as he settled between the silken prison of her thighs. His eyes lifted once again to stare into the slumberous depths of hers, and he smiled then, a smile that filled her heart until she thought it would burst.

He bent his head so that his breath mingled with hers. "Oh, Samantha...I was wrong." His whisper was hoarse against her mouth, his breath harsh and rasping. "So wrong. This is—heaven on earth."

And then there were no more words as they were both swept away on a cloud of passion, a whirling giddy feeling overtaking them both. His body surged boldly against hers, yet mingled within that thrusting urgency was an aching tenderness that moved her to tears.

Much later when their breathing had returned to normal, Jason lifted his head to look down at her. That same tender smile curved his mouth as he finally swept aside the bedspread and blankets and scooped her under them. Scarcely wanting to move from the lethargy that followed their fiery union, she lifted a finger to trace the shape of his lips, reveling in their smooth texture.

The pad of his thumb came up to trace the path of the single tear that had slid down her cheek. "Regrets, already?" he asked softly.

Samantha shook her head swiftly, still awed by what had happened. Even loving Alan as she had, she had never felt such all-consuming passion, such immense satisfaction and utter peacefulness. "Not at all," she said softly, her blue eyes shining. "I—I've never felt quite like this," she added with a touch of shyness.

Jason bent to brush her lips. "Neither have I, sweetheart," he said huskily, his arms tightening around her. "Neither have I."

In spite of herself, Samantha tensed a little. "Not even with your ex-wife..."

She broke off, afraid for a second she had shattered the magical bond between them, but although there was a guarded expression in his eyes for an instant, it disappeared as he saw her wariness.

"I'll tell you something, Samantha," he said quietly. "I never loved my wife, not really. Oh, I thought I did, but it didn't take me long to discover that it was no more than infatuation." He hesitated, and she knew the words were forced from deep inside him. "Natalie came to L.A. like a thousand other women, with visions of stardom dancing in her head. You remember I told you I was a sitcom writer for a while?"

Samantha nodded, listening intently. She sensed this might be the one and only time Jason would ever talk of his ex-wife.

"Natalie was beautiful, ambitious and very vain." His voice hardened. "She's a woman who needs constant adoration, and it wasn't long before I found out a husband didn't stop her from sleeping with any man who wanted her. Believe me, there were plenty. When I found out, I divorced her, and she told me afterward that the only reason she married me in the first place was because of my contacts in the industry."

"How sad." Samantha's eyes moved over the faintly bitter lines of his face. She wanted to reach out and touch him, smooth them away with her fingers, but she wasn't sure if he would welcome her touch right now. So she stayed where she was, her head on the pillow next to his. But not before a question slipped out. "Is she a big star right now?"

Jason shook his head. "She does a commercial now and then but she's a lousy actress. Freeloading is her present specialty."

Samantha frowned and turned to look at him. "Is that why you were going to L.A. to see your attorney?"

Again he nodded. "She's been trying to get her hands on some property I bought during the divorce proceedings." A hard little smile curved his lips. "But as it turned out, the matter was dismissed because she eloped with a French director. Now she's his problem."

He turned on his side to face her, his hand resting possessively on her stomach. He smiled a little crookedly. "Now it's your turn. Why did things go sour with Alex?"

Samantha smiled slightly. "It's Alan, not Alex," she reminded him. "And I'm not sure I can say what went wrong. It just didn't work out. Maybe we didn't take the time to get to know each other well enough. Believe it or not, Alan and I got married exactly three weeks after we met."

Jason raised an eyebrow. "That is amazing." He regarded her quietly. "Do you still love him, Samantha?"

She turned sideways so that she faced him, the sheet draped loosely over her body. Her heart leaped as she saw the guarded expression in his eyes. She had the oddest sensation that it really mattered to him.

She ran a hand down his chest, twining her fingers in the narrowing trail of curls on his lean stomach. "No," she said softly. She gazed into his eyes. "The magic just didn't last."

Jason raised an eyebrow. "That's quite an admission coming from a woman who thinks love is an endless bed of roses."

"Maybe you were right and I *did* expect too much of it. I suppose, thinking back, that neither one of us was ready to sacrifice. Alan was just getting started in his job, and I was working on my master's at Portland State." She sighed reflectively. "When things began looking bad, I suppose I did what every woman does. I blamed him, and then I blamed myself. But the truth is—" and she was beginning to realize it now more than ever, though she didn't say so "—Alan wasn't the right man for me." Her eyes met his. "But we're still friends."

"I noticed," he commented dryly.

She smiled at him. "Now don't you feel better that we've both got all the skeletons out of the closet?"

Jason's grin was both devilish and lovable. The realization tore at her heart as she was gathered closely in his arms. Lovable—how easily the admission came. She loved this man, right or wrong. Lord, how she loved him!

His hand swept aside the sheet with a single movement. Their bodies lay bare to each other's gaze. "I only wish we'd done it a long time ago." His husky tone was tinged with amusement, but his smile faded as he looked into her eyes. "Samantha, would you believe me if I told you I didn't plan what just happened?"

Her heart melted at his searching look. Her hands slid around to twine in the thick hair on his nape. "Yes," she said simply. "Oh, yes!"

"I won't say I wasn't hoping." A faintly teasing light reappeared in his eyes, but his mouth was tender as his lips sought hers. "But I knew you needed some time."

"Jason, you gave me all the time I needed." And as his hands skimmed over her body, the exquisitely fulfilling passion flared anew between them. This time she knew it could last forever.

It made her just a little sad.

"Jason! Jason Armstrong! Dammit, are you still in bed? You lazy old son of a—"

The good-natured male voice dropped off as Samantha abruptly sat up in bed, clutching the sheet to her bare breasts. Sunlight streamed through the drapes, silhouetting a man standing in the bedroom doorway.

"Jason!" Her elbow nudged his bare shoulder, rising just above the sheet, her startled eyes still on the figure lounging against the doorjamb. He was in his mid-thirties, roughly Jason's age, with wavy chestnut hair and sparkling blue eyes. "Jason, wake up!" He finally stirred at her hushed whisper and, to her horror, pressed a warm kiss on the silken thigh near his face. His hand delved beneath the sheet and sought the smooth hollow of her stomach, his fingers straying relentlessly downward.

"Jason, get up!" She scooted as far away from him as she could. Dear Lord, to wake from a delightful passionate night in heaven—to this!

"I think you'd better, Jason. I've never seen a face so fiery red in all my life."

The strange laughing voice at last roused Jason. Dark hair tousled from sleep, he sat up and stared at the intruder. He broke into a grin. "Dave! I didn't think you were coming until Friday."

"I can see that," the stranger commented, returning his grin.

Heedless of his nakedness, Jason sat up in bed and stretched. He ran a hand through his hair, then curled an arm around Samantha, who resisted the effort by pulling the sheet up to her nose and sliding down onto the pillows.

"Don't be rude now, Samantha. This is my long-time friend and buddy, David Winters." She cringed at the smile in his voice. "David, meet your neighbor, Samantha Monroe."

To her horror, David Winters acknowledged the greeting gravely. "It's nice to finally meet you, Samantha. I'd say the pleasure was all mine but obviously it hasn't been." She peeked over the sheet to find him smiling. "If I'd known what I was missing, I'd have made the trip much sooner."

This time she did moan. Turning her face into the pillow, she muttered half-miserably, half-angrily,

"Jason, will you get him out of here so I can go home?"

"So soon?" He looked genuinely surprised. "Don't you even want breakfast?" He grinned at David. "As I recall, Dave can whip up a mean batch of pancakes."

When she raised her head enough to glare at him, he nodded at his friend, a crooked grin etching his lean features. David obligingly left the room. He grinned as Samantha got up from the bed, draping the sheet around her body. "No need to be so modest," he teased lightly. "You weren't last night." He sighed when Samantha fixed him with another blistering stare. "We'll meet you downstairs."

When he had slipped into a pair of jeans, she stalked to the bathroom, where her sunsuit and underwear were draped over the shower door. After dressing hurriedly she slipped out through the bedroom onto the upper deck. Her face burned with both anger and embarrassment at the thought of facing those two laughing faces. Five minutes later she was back in her own house and in the shower.

The stinging spray washed over her body with a thoroughness that reminded her of the long fiery night spent in Jason's arms, his hands sliding intimately over every inch of her body, exploring and arousing her to heights she'd only dreamed of before. Such sweet devastating pleasure was beyond anything she'd ever known. His desire for her had been boundless, exciting—as was hers for him. How many times had they made love? Too many to count. And each fiery taking had left her passionately fulfilled, but she turned breathlessly, eagerly, in his arms at each renewed caress.

She closed her eyes against the memory. What next, she thought dully, turning to rinse her back. Would Jason think she was ripe for the picking any time he wanted—for as long as he was here? She didn't know, and that was the whole problem. If his lighthearted attitude this morning had been any indication . . .

She sighed and reached for a towel. She couldn't help but think of his sweet husky whispers in her ear all through the night. She could have sworn she was special.

"Damn it, Samantha, when are you going to wake up and separate reality from fantasy?" she scolded herself irritably. "It didn't mean a damn thing to him—no more than a purely physical release—while it meant the world to you!"

But facts were facts, and it had happened. There would be no going back, and she was simply going to have to accept it. The only problem was how. How did a woman go about forgetting a man who only happened once in a lifetime?

She was still pondering that question when Jason walked into the kitchen and found her toying with a half-eaten bowl of cereal that had been poured an hour before.

"Samantha." His voice roused her from her lethargy as he sat down across from her. "Why didn't you stay and eat breakfast with us?"

She took a sip of her coffee and grimaced at the bitter taste. It was cold. "You know why," she muttered without looking at him.

"You felt awkward." His voice was very gentle.

She raised her head long enough to send him a burning gaze. "You may be used to being caught in bed by David Winters but I'm not!"

"That was a first," he said softly. "The last day has brought a lot of firsts—for both of us."

Samantha didn't dare question that self-satisfied smile. Not only did she understand his meaning only too well, it brought up a subject that she suspected was best left alone.

"You didn't like David, did you?"

"We didn't meet under the best of circumstances," she said evasively.

"I agree," he murmured thoughtfully. "It's too bad he's gone back to Portland already. He really is a good friend and I think you'd have liked him."

Her mouth tightened. "I'm not so sure!" she retorted. "From what you've told me and what I saw, you two are a lot alike—both after a good time!"

Jason's eyes darkened suddenly. His hands reached across the table and pinned one of hers. His eyes scrutinized hers intensely. "You think that's all last night meant to me—a good time?"

Samantha pulled her hand back abruptly, ignoring the shock that went through her. She didn't want him to touch her—not now, not yet. She wished she had his ability to make light of any and every situation but right now all she wanted to do was cry. She averted her eyes and carried her cup and bowl to the sink. Silently she rinsed them, aware of Jason's eyes on her back. She gripped the counter tightly.

"I—I've never... you're only the second man I've ever..."

"Made love with?" Jason came to stand behind her. His hands on her shoulders were oddly comforting, despite the fact that he was the sole source of her unease. "Once I found out you'd been married, did you think I didn't know that?" His warm breath stirred her hair. "You're a rare breed, Samantha.

There aren't many women left like you. There aren't *enough* like you."

There was something elusive about those words, something hidden just below the surface. She couldn't grasp it at the moment. There was too much going on inside her, too many conflicting emotions. But Jason's voice was like warm honey flowing over her. She wasn't aware of the tight coil of tension inside her until she relaxed a little.

He pulled her back until she leaned against him willingly. His arms slipped around her waist, the slender line of her back fit snugly against the solid warmth of his chest, and her head fell back naturally against the place where his shoulder joined his neck.

"Are you still embarrassed about David walking in on us?"

"He probably thinks I'm the type to fall in bed with just anybody," she muttered. "He knows you've only been here a few weeks, Jason!"

A soft laugh sounded in her ear. "Anyone who took the time to know you would realize you would never do something so—" she could feel his smile against her cheek "—so impulsive."

"And now you're making fun of me again!" she grumbled. "He might be your friend but I'm glad he's gone. I don't think I could even look him in the eye!"

Jason turned her to face him, his hands resting lightly on her waist. "For all your reading on the subject of sex—" he teased lightly "—you're not very worldly. Not that I'd change a thing about you," he added hastily on seeing her mouth open.

Samantha finally relented and smiled. "That's different—there's no one in the room with me!"

He laughed and brushed his lips over her forehead, his eyes twinkling. "I have the perfect solution should

David ever arrive so unexpectedly again," he said smoothly.

Her mouth turned down at the corners. "And that is?"

His eyes traveled slowly over her face before coming to rest on her mouth. His own was no longer smiling. "Marry me, Samantha," he said softly. "Marry me."

Ten

———

Shock rippled through her in wave after wave. Samantha opened her mouth, then closed it, and opened it again, feeling like a puppet whose string was being pulled. He sounded perfectly serious, she thought in amazement, and yet he couldn't be.

She walked into the living room and sat down on the sofa numbly. It couldn't be happening—and yet it was. "This is silly," she thought with a shake of her head.

"Silly?" She wasn't even aware that she had spoken until Jason dropped down beside her. "You call it silly when a man asks you to marry him?"

Samantha stared at him. "Yes, silly!" she protested. "Someone walks in and finds us in bed together and you ask me to marry you? It—it's just like something out of one of your books—" she waved her hands in the air "—where the characters only get married because of duty...or honor."

"As you once pointed out, my heroes aren't usually very honorable—especially at first. And they are never, and I repeat never, forced to do something against their will, even though it might take them a while to realize it," he assured her gravely, a faint light twinkling in his eyes.

"But that doesn't have a thing to do with us!" A faint suspicion stirred inside her. "Are you playing games with me again?" she demanded hotly. "All along you've been setting me up...that bit about being a hero with your big rescue scene, playing at being a modern-day Romeo, sending all those balloons, trying to soften me up with all those lovesick lines!"

She jumped to her feet and glared at him. "Did you decide to single me out just to have a little fun? Did you pick on me because I'm so—so damned sentimental?"

"Samantha, you're taking this all wrong." He chuckled a little as he dragged her down beside him. Arms like bands of steel wrapped tightly around her rigid form. She knew from experience there was little use in trying to get away from him. She wasn't sure if she was more angry or hurt, but to her distress, hot angry tears burned her throat.

"Maybe you'd prefer the more traditional approach." The next thing she knew Jason was down on his knees before her, one of her icy hands clamped tightly in both of his. "Will you marry me, Samantha?"

All her anger fled at his soft words. "Why...why are you doing this?" she asked weakly.

"Why?" His fingers traced a sensitive pattern on the inside of her wrist. "You just accused me of being a Romeo—and it's true. After what Natalie did to me I didn't want any kind of serious relationship with a woman. And then I met you. You were different, right from the start. You're all the things I forgot existed in a woman. You're sweet and innocent and yet you're the sexiest lady I've ever known. But you're also the strongest woman I know.''

Samantha shook her head in protest. ''I'm not—''

His fingers against her mouth stifled the words. ''You are.'' He smiled rather crookedly. ''Not many women could watch their marriage end in divorce and survive with all their romantic ideals intact. You're a winner, a survivor.''

Her lips trembled. If she was so strong, why was she filled with such fear? Such doubt and uncertainty? ''Jason...''

''Remember when we met, and you said you expected fireworks and skyrockets, and maybe even a few shooting stars?'' She nodded slowly. ''I feel that way every time I look at you,'' he said quietly. ''I light up inside whenever I'm with you.'' His eyes were very soft as he looked at her. ''You're in my every thought, Samantha. The way you look—your eyes, your mouth.'' His fingers gently caressed her features. ''The way you feel, so soft and sweet whenever I hold you.'' One finger slid down to trace the shape of her breast, circling with exquisite tenderness around the throbbing peak.

Her body tightened at the caress, and her throat swelled shut. She was too full of emotion to speak.

''Be the keeper of my heart, Samantha,'' he urged softly. ''Marry me.''

Her eyes clung to his. She saw the world reflected in those clear brown depths—her dreams and her fantasies, her hopes and her prayers. She choked off a half-sob. The words were like a treasure trove of gold and diamonds, but unless they came straight from the heart, they meant nothing. If only that odd half-smile weren't playing about his lips. If only she could believe he meant every word he said.

But where did the writer end and the man begin?

She didn't know. Heaven help her, she didn't know.

"Jason." Her voice shook. This was a dream, an illusion. It couldn't be happening. She pulled gently away from his grasp and rose numbly. Before she knew it she was running blindly to the bedroom and pulling a suitcase from the closet.

"Samantha."

"What?" She scarcely heard his voice over the thundering of her heart. She opened a dresser drawer and, pulling out a handful of underwear, threw it into the open case.

"What are you doing?" His voice, for all its quietness, was utterly demanding. He was no longer smiling.

"What does it look like? I'm packing."

"Why?"

"Does it matter?" She whirled around to face him. "You come and go as you please—can't I?"

The merest suggestion of a smile lifted his lips. "This is rather—sudden." He picked up a scrap of silk that had fallen to the floor. It made her heart ache when she saw it was the underwear dotted with hearts that had caught his attention the day after they met. It seemed years ago.

"Rather sudden?" She gave a slightly hysterical laugh. "That's supposed to be my line."

"Where are you going, Samantha?"

She shook her head. "I don't know—anywhere. Anywhere away from you." There was a stunned silence, and she looked up at Jason, her eyes a little wild. A flash of hurt crossed his face, and his eyes were dark with bewilderment.

"Oh, God, I'm sorry," she muttered. She sat down on the bed and lifted shaking hands to her temples. Marriage—to Jason! She should have been elated, ecstatic! But all she could think was that he was absolutely crazy! She could only repeat what was racing through her mind. The words tumbled out in a rush. "I didn't expect this from you. The last thing I expected was a marriage proposal!"

He sat down beside her, but must have sensed her desire not to have him touch her. If he had, she felt as if she'd shatter into a million pieces!

"Don't you know what you want, Samantha?" He gave her a long searching look.

"Yes...no!" she said shakily. "Oh, damn! Right now I don't feel I even know myself very well, let alone what I want!" She raised pleading eyes to his. "Please, I just need some time to think this through, and I can't do it with you around."

Jason studied her for a very long time. "All right," he finally said slowly, apparently satisfied with what he saw. "But I want to know where you'll be."

She took a deep, steadying breath. "I'll be at my mother's." She watched as he started toward the door. "Jason...you'll be here when I get back?" She couldn't stop the quaver in her voice.

The room grew very still, but the air was suddenly leaping with currents. Samantha didn't realize how tightly she gripped the edge of the mattress until she heard his voice.

"I'll be here," he promised gravely.

Her mother was pleasantly surprised to see her again so soon. "Samantha! My goodness, you just left a week ago!" Lillian Reed laughed. "Aren't you a little old to be homesick so much?"

Samantha took one look at her warm welcoming smile and burst into tears.

Five days later there were no more tears left, but she was no nearer a decision about marrying Jason, either. She was afraid to say no, and even more afraid to say yes.

He'd walked her to her car the day she left, looking strangely somber. She had felt guilty as she noticed the deepening grooves near his mouth, the faint lines above his forehead. She knew her reaction had surprised him as much as his proposal had stunned her.

She could hear her mother bustling around in the kitchen, finishing the after-dinner dishes, the opening and closing of cupboard doors. Familiar sounds, comforting sounds. She looked around the small living room of the two-bedroom bungalow she and her mother had shared after her father had made his final disappearance—the cushioned chintz-covered chairs, the old rocking chair draped with an afghan near the fireplace, the small oak desk where she'd diligently studied for all her high-school exams. This house had been the first place she had ever really called home, and she'd always felt a special kind of peacefulness and security here in this room.

Until now. Now there was a strange restlessness inside her that wouldn't be denied.

She sighed and joined her mother in the kitchen where she was pouring a fresh cup of coffee for both of them.

Lillian sat down across from her. "You know you're going to have to give Jason an answer sooner or later," she said quietly, then gave her daughter an odd look. "You shouldn't avoid it any longer."

Samantha smiled half-heartedly. "I never thought I'd see the day when you were trying to get rid of me."

"Not trying to get rid of you, dear, only trying to make you see the light."

She sighed and curled her hands around her cup. "You don't understand, mom," she began carefully. The two of them had had a rather long talk the night she'd arrived—or rather she had alternately talked and cried, and her mother had listened and comforted.

"Oh, I think I do." Her mother regarded her quietly. "You think if you wait long enough to give him an answer, he'll go back to California and then you can blame him for everything that went wrong."

Samantha started. "That's not true—" she began to protest, then stopped short. Was it? Maybe she didn't want to make a choice, end up regretting it, and then have no one to blame but herself.

"You don't trust him, do you? You don't trust him enough to believe in him."

Maybe she was right, Samantha acknowledged wearily. She stared pensively past the crisply starched yellow curtains hanging at the window to the aging Victorian house next door. Two small boys were playing on the front porch, running down the steps and racing their tricycles over the sidewalk and back to the porch again. Their chatter could be heard through the open window.

"You see that, mom?" She pointed suddenly toward the two youngsters. "That's what I want for me, and for my family—if and when I ever have one. I want to know my kids are happy and secure, and that they won't wake up one morning and find they only have one parent left."

Her mother looked at her strangely. "And you think that will happen if you marry Jason?"

A lump formed in her throat. "I don't know," she whispered. "And I'm not sure I want to take the chance. He—he's a lot like...like dad." She swallowed painfully. "Always on the move." She shook her head. "I don't want to live like that again."

"And you don't want to be like me—married one day and abandoned the next."

Samantha nodded miserably. Her mother's hands reached out to cover hers. "I think it's time I shared something with you that I should have told you a long time ago." Her mother's voice was very quiet. "Your father was an adventurer, a dreamer, just like you." She smiled gently. "But he was almost a child at heart, Samantha. He couldn't separate his dreams from reality. He could never be satisfied for long. But that didn't mean he stopped loving you the day he walked out of our lives—"

"Didn't it?" Her voice was slightly bitter. "He never came back—and that says it all."

Lillian shook her head. "He would have—if I'd let him."

Samantha looked at her strangely. "What do you mean?"

"I still loved your father when he left, only I couldn't live with him any longer." The laugh her mother gave sounded oddly strangled. "Or maybe I should say I couldn't live *like* that, and neither could you. You worshiped him, and I couldn't let him come back into your life, build your hopes up, and then walk out on you again." She smiled, a rather sad little smile. "He'd have taken us with him that time too, only after all those years I was tired of chasing after the moon. I don't regret the years I spent with your father, they were happy ones, but I've learned we make our own happiness. The pot of gold at the end of the rainbow is only as far as we make it, Samantha, only as far as we make it.''

Samantha looked at her mother a long time. "I'm not sure I understand," she said slowly. "Are you saying Jason isn't like...my father?"

Her mother shook her head quickly. "All I'm saying is give it a chance," she said quietly. "The years I spent with your father were among the best—and yes, the worst. But if I had it to do over again I'd probably make the same choice."

Her mother talked of reality. Of dreams. Of chasing the moon. But wasn't it true that if she thought anything would come of herself and Jason she'd be living in a fool's paradise? She clung stubbornly to the thought. He'd said she was different. How long would it be before the novelty wore off and he grew bored with her? For all his handsomeness, his charm, that delightfully teasing smile she'd come to love so much, Jason had one fatal flaw—his disbelief in love. And hers? Hers was in loving a man like him.

"Do you love him, Samantha?"

"I...yes."

"Do you need him?"

She didn't want to think about a long lonely winter without Jason, but she did now. The thought was like a knife in her heart.

A lump in her throat, she nodded. When her mother opened her mouth, she anticipated the next question and made a sound that was a cross between a laugh and a sob. "Please don't ask if I want him!"

Her mother smiled. "I wasn't going to," she said calmly. "I'm simply going to ask you for the last time what you're doing here. It seems to me you should be telling Jason this!''

Samantha shook her head. ''Maybe he thinks he wants me now, but what about tomorrow? What about next year? If you could only see him—he could have any woman in the world!''

''And you think it won't last.'' Her mother held up a hand. ''No, you're afraid it won't last.''

She nodded, too miserable to speak, but her thoughts delved backward. Jason had told her that her kind of love was white knights and fairy tales, but wasn't it about time she realized that nothing, love included, was perfect? But that didn't mean it didn't exist, she argued with herself. Love between a man and a woman was a need, a partnership, and involved caring and commitment, and something she and Alan had never been able to achieve—give-and-take.

She let the realization wash over her, and felt a dawning sense of awareness. She didn't want a perfect man after all, the fantasy man she had always dreamed of. She wanted a man who was secure enough in his masculinity to love with all his heart without being afraid to share the same joy and pain as she, someone who was sensitive and vulnerable, a man who loved as intensely as she did. And hadn't Jason pointed out the first day they'd met that men were really no different than women? *And wasn't he all of those things?*

But doubt was a dark cloud overhead that wasn't as easily banished as she hoped.

Lillian got up and brushed a kiss against her forehead. ''You know what I think?'' she asked softly. ''I think the only one you're hurting is yourself if you let yourself believe he's not the man for you.''

''But—you don't even know him!''

"You'd be surprised, dear." Lillian walked into the living room and returned with a copy of *Love's Sweet Bondage* in her hand. "I found this on your bureau a few days ago and I finally decided to see what the big attraction was." She laid it in Samantha's lap. "And in reading it I discovered quite a lot about Cathryn James—or rather Jason Armstrong." She shook her head. "If I were twenty years younger..." She stopped, her eyes gleaming, her meaning clear. "Why don't you read it, Samantha—read it and think of the man who wrote it."

Those were strange words indeed coming from her mother, who usually read no more than the newspaper or an occasional magazine, Samantha reflected later in her bedroom. She smiled a little ruefully as she picked up the copy of *Love's Sweet Bondage* and eyed Sabrina's voluptuous form draped around Marshall's chest. She didn't even know why she'd brought it along, but maybe getting involved in Sabrina's troubles with the roguish Marshall would get her mind off Jason, if only for a while....

She ended up crying herself to sleep again that night, only this time it was different. They were tears of happiness.

Samantha's little car crunched to a grinding halt in her own driveway early the next evening. Her sandaled feet hit the pavement, the pale yellow skirt she wore whipping around her bare legs as she raced across the pathway to Jason's house, her feet scarcely touching the ground.

Jason. The thought of his gently teasing grin, his warm brown eyes, whether dancing with humor or aflame with passion, filled her heart with warmth and hope and love unlike anything she had ever known.

Last night had been such a revelation. For the first time, she saw him clearly for the man he was—the man she wanted, the man who was hers. There were no more doubts, no lingering insecurities that made her fear the future.

She smiled to herself as she lifted a finger to press the doorbell. Her heart threatened to burst with the warm buoyant feeling inside her. She pictured the welcome she knew was only seconds away. Jason would be surprised, since she hadn't bothered to phone. But then he would smile, that warm, heart-rending smile that never failed to send her heart melting with emotion and her blood sizzling through her veins.

It was then that she noticed the silence. She shoved aside the anxious feeling that swelled inside her and rang the doorbell again. She heard its lonely peal, heard it echo through the house.

No one answered.

It wasn't until then that a cold feeling of dread began to penetrate the bubble around her heart. His car—Jason's car was gone! Scarcely daring to breathe, she ran around to the back and onto the deck. She peered through the woven draperies . . . the house was empty as a tomb. For an instant she refused to accept it, then she felt the world come crashing down around her ears. It was happening, she thought wildly, a strange buzzing in her head. What she had feared all along was actually happening . . . Jason was gone . . . *gone*.

For a minute she thought she'd stopped breathing. Then she heard a harsh gasping sound and realized it came from her own throat.

"You promised," she whispered brokenly. *"You promised."*

Eleven

———

Samantha."

She reeled at the sound behind her; then, like a child seeking shelter from a storm, she ran straight into Jason's arms. He caught her up against him and held her there, his arms closing around her trembling figure.

"Jason!" Her voice broke on a sob. "I thought you were gone! I thought you left me!" Her eyes closed and she buried her face against his bare chest, tickling her cheek on the rough dark hairs sprinkled beneath the base of his throat.

"Samantha." His hand smoothed the ruffled wings of her hair. "I was on the beach. If you'd tried the door you'd have found it open."

She smiled tremulously at him, her eyes clinging to his. She stepped back but wouldn't let loose his hands, keeping them linked between their bodies. She shook her head. "Your car..."

"Is in the garage, where it's been since you left."
His eyes seemed to devour her, the warmly possessive
light she saw there making her heart pound madly.

She laughed a little breathlessly. "You're reverting
to your old habits, I see." She nodded at his khaki-
colored shorts, his only attire.

"Only because I had a feeling you'd be back today." His grin was faintly teasing as he tugged gently
on her hands. "Come on, I'll show you where I was."

Her hand tucked firmly inside his, they walked
down to the beach, their bodies occasionally touching. Samantha could feel something different, a new
closeness, a new feeling of kinship between them. She
thrilled at the feeling.

She smiled when he finally stopped. The sand at
their feet was molded into a castle, almost an exact
replica of the one they had labored over nearly a week
earlier. "Is this what you've been doing while I've
been gone?" she teased. "I thought you'd have your
manuscript finished by now."

Jason smiled. "We don't have much history, you
and I. But the day we spent here was a day I'll never
forget as long as I live." He thumped his chest with a
fist. "Haven't you learned yet that I'm a romantic at
heart—" he glanced at her out of the corner of his eye
"—dreaming of lordly castles and damsels in distress?" He added so softly she could scarcely hear,
"How could I write when my inspiration was gone—
and she hadn't yet returned?"

A warm feeling welled up inside her. She tipped her
head to the side and sank down to her knees, heedless
of the damage the damp sand might do to her skirt.
"This looks exactly like the other one."

"It should, it had the same crew." One side of his
mouth turned up and he added dryly, "I think by now
every kid that's ever played on this beach knows me as

'Mr. Monroe.'" He looked at her then, the expression in his eyes growing more intense, and she could see the silent question in his eyes.

She stilled it with a pleading look, clasping her hands together tightly in her lap. That could wait, this couldn't. "Jason, I finally finished *Love's Sweet Bondage*."

"And?" His voice was cautious.

"And—I love it, even more than I loved all the others. But for a very different reason."

Jason looked puzzled.

Samantha smiled a little. She didn't possess his eloquence when it came to words. "When we first met, you said the kind of love that was depicted in romance novels didn't exist—"

"I didn't say that," he interrupted with a frown. "I said it was exaggerated." His hand found hers where it lay on her lap. "And I believed it—at the time."

A twinge of regret flashed in the blue eyes that met his. "And I thought it wasn't possible for you to ever change—until last night."

"And reading *Love's Sweet Bondage* changed your mind?"

She nodded. "Suddenly I realized something all your books have in common—fidelity, and the concept of everlasting love. The hero and heroine never make love with anyone else, and I like that." She paused. "I believe in that, Jason, and I've finally learned that we make our own magic. But I also believe in fidelity. And I believe that forever *can* happen—for the right people. And for the first time, I read between the lines." She leaned forward, her eyes searching his face. "Do you know what else I found, Jason?"

There was a dawning look in Jason's eyes, as if he was just beginning to understand what she was trying to say. His hand tightened around hers.

"I found that I was right after all," she said with a note of wonderment in her voice. "That a good writer puts a part of herself—" she smiled and glanced down at where their fingers were entwined in her lap "—I guess I should say himself, into everything he does." Her smile was both sweet and a trifle impish as her eyes lifted. "My guess is that every romance you've ever written has been a little fantasy of your own."

Jason shook his head, his smile playfully rueful. "How could I have ever accused such a down-to-earth woman of being a dreamer?" Something flickered in the back of his eyes, and the teasing light faded. "I tried to tell you how I felt about you," he said huskily. "Especially the day I asked you to marry me."

"I know that now," she admitted. "I heard, but I didn't listen. I didn't listen here—" she laid her free hand on her heart, and her voice dropped tremulously "—where I should have. And you said everything I wanted to hear, everything but the one thing I *needed* to hear."

"Everything but I love you."

The placid statement was maddening. There was a heartbeat of silence while Samantha's heart throbbed fearfully. She knew, and there was a part of her that still needed to hear the words, wanted it with every fiber of her body. Her body tensed as she waited . . .

"I do, you know."

His tone was chiding, almost amused. She drew a shallow breath, her eyes two huge pools of longing as they rested on Jason's face. For once his smile was almost imperceptible. "You do—what?"

"I do love you." This time the words were as husky and shaky as she felt inside. Samantha knew a brief wild joy and then she was being dragged across Jason's lap, cradled in his arms as if he would never let her go. "God, how I love you," he ground out against her mouth, her hair, her cheeks, over and over again. He allowed himself one long searing kiss and then eased back from her gently. "I would have told you then if I thought you'd have believed me," he said. "Instead I tried to let you know every other way I knew how—the night we made love, when I asked you to marry me."

Samantha shook her head, still rather dazed. She had finally realized it last night, but hearing the hunger in his words, seeing the tenderness in his eyes . . . "I wish you'd told me then," she choked out.

He drew back from her slightly so he could see her face. "You had to find out for yourself," he said gently.

"Jason," she said, hesitating, "I was so mixed up."

"Shhh." He kissed her lips tenderly. "You don't have to explain. I understand, I really do." He gave a shaky laugh. "It sure took you long enough to sort it all through. This last week has been hell!"

"For me, too," she admitted. Her eyes grew misty. "I was afraid to read too much into everything you said. I thought you were teasing me, that it was just a game."

"Sweetheart, it stopped being a game almost from the minute I pulled you up from the sand and gazed into those beautiful blue eyes of yours." He laughed as shakily as she. "You looked at me as if you were star struck and I felt like I'd been hit on the head with a ten-pound mallet." His hand trespassed beneath the hem of her skirt. "Are you a one-man woman?" he asked huskily.

She shivered beneath the magic his fingers were making as they traced a languorous path up her thigh. "Are you a one-woman man?"

"You have to ask that after reading all of my books?" He gave her an admonishing grin. "And you still haven't given me an answer—are you or are you not going to marry me?"

She tightened her arms around his neck, her eyes shining. "Somehow I just can't seem to say no to you."

"Is that a yes?"

She laughed softly, seductively, and eased back so that he followed her down. The sand was soft and cushiony beneath her back, the weight of his body on hers warm and secure. She closed her eyes and arched her body sinuously against his, feeling the heat rising in his body and responding to it instinctively.

"Hey! Hey, Miss Monroe!"

The piping little voice came from directly behind them. Jason buried his face in her throat and muttered, "This is beginning to become a habit. That young man had better learn a few things about timing or he may never reach an age where he's able to make use of it!"

Samantha suppressed a smile and slipped from beneath Jason's body. Kevin was still apparently impervious to the scene he had interrupted—again. Wearing an ear-splitting grin, he hopped up and down in excitement.

"Guess what, Miss Monroe, Mr. Monroe." He bobbed his head in a greeting as Jason sat up and ran a hand through his rumpled dark hair. "Me and my little sister get to go camping with my uncle next week! We get to help put up the tent, and take our own sleeping bags . . . ain't that neat?"

"That *does* sound exciting," she assured him, resisting the bubble of laughter that threatened to erupt at Jason's disgruntled expression. "You can tell the class about it next year during show-and-tell." She nodded over at Jason. "By the way, Kevin, I think you should know that this isn't Mr. Monroe, his name is Mr. Armstrong—"

"And in a very short time—" Jason's lean features had suddenly transformed into a grin "—*Miss* Monroe is going to become *Mrs*. Armstrong. Spread the word among your buddies so they know when September rolls around, will you, pal?"

Samantha's eyes sparkled as they met his. "You took the words right out of my mouth. And I do *so* love a masterful man," she teased. Brushing the sand off her skirt, she got up and held out a hand to him. "How would you feel about a little show-and-tell of our own?"

He was on his feet in the blink of an eye. "And I do *so* love an aggressive woman," he crooned tenderly.

They had a hard time keeping their eyes, as well as their hands, off each other during the short trek back to the house. Always before with Jason, she had felt as if she had been on the outside looking in with a faint gray film between them, afraid to let herself see him for the man he really was. But for the first time, she recognized the glow in his eyes for what it was—love, a love so tender and sweet it made her ache inside.

The feeling was as thrilling as it was arousing. They had no sooner entered the bedroom than Samantha turned in his arms and lifted her face to his, pressing her body urgently into his as she tangled her fingers in the crisp hair at his nape.

Jason laughed delightedly at her eagerness. "Is this a preview of nights to come?"

His hands had already wandered to the buttons of her short linen shirt. She shivered as he undid the clasp of her bra and her breasts spilled free, the budding tips already hard and erect. Her skirt was the next to go, dropped in a careless pool at her feet. She pressed herself boldly against his naked chest in a sinuous motion that sent Jason's breath rattling in his throat. "You bring out the wild and wanton in me," she said with a seductive laugh.

His eyes glittered fiercely as he threaded his hands in her hair and brought her face to his. He took her mouth in a hotly passionate kiss.

Her head was spinning when he released her. His breath fanned hotly against her cheek. His desire pressed urgently against the fluid lines of her belly and she thrilled that she was able to arouse him to such an extent. Emboldened by the knowledge, she let the sensitive tips of her fingers wander down the fabric of his shorts, tracing the stunning male shape of him in a blatantly sensual caress.

"What about you?" she taunted softly. "What do I bring out in you?"

Jason stepped out of his shorts and grasped her hips to bring her in line with his body in one fluid movement. "The savage beast unleashed?" he suggested with a soft rumble of laughter in his chest.

"An apt analogy," he agreed with a meaningful glance down his body. But the laughter lurking in her voice faded as her eyes made their way lingeringly up the taut lines of his body. Dappled sunlight glinted through the windows and shimmered on the copper-hued flesh, bringing to vivid life the sheer latent power beneath the smoothly flowing muscles.

Desire rose hotly in Samantha's veins, but she had a need far more intense, far more lasting, and much more powerful.

Her hands lifted to tangle in the crisp dark hair at his nape. "Make love to me, Jason," she said simply. "Make love to me."

He bent to lift her gently in his arms. "With pleasure," he groaned in her sweet-smelling hair. "With pleasure...."

And the wild union that followed was like nothing Samantha had ever dreamed of, or even imagined. He touched, he stroked, he tasted and caressed every part of her body as if to imprint the image of it on his brain forever. Then he allowed her the same intimate knowledge of his supple male strength, until at last he moved over her trembling body. Then at the last moment, he rolled so that she was poised over him.

"Your trusty steed awaits, m'lady," he said hoarsely, his eyes locked with hers endlessly. Awed by the golden glow in his eyes and the boundless sweetness of his tormenting fingers, she couldn't look away as he guided her yielding body downward. She moaned deliriously as her softness closed over his thrusting hardness.

A tormented groan of pure pleasure tore from Jason's throat, and Samantha found herself caught up in the sheer joy of it. At first he rocked against her gently, his hands on her hips, as if to savor and prolong the moment, until neither one could stand the sweetly restrained pace. Their bodies surged and met with an increasing power and driving urgency that sent them stealing out and away to the heavens and beyond.

They reached that pinnacle of feeling at one and the same moment, each crying the other's name until it receded into a breathless whisper of sound. Their breath intertwined, they lay basking in a warmth that went far beyond the immense physical satisfaction they had just known.

Curled up in the haven of his arms, Samantha turned her face and pressed a kiss against his collar-bone. "I love you," she whispered softly.

Jason looked down at her. "Lady, I was beginning to wonder," he drawled with a grin. It faded to a smile, and the light in his eyes grew softer yet. "I've been waiting a lifetime for a woman like you." He bent and brushed her lips. "By the way, I have something to tell you."

Samantha snuggled closer against him. "What?"

"I bought this house."

"You what?" Disbelief edged her voice, and her hand stilled its restless roaming against his chest. "When?"

Jason grinned. "Why do you think David came down last week?"

She propped herself on an elbow and stared at him in amazement. "Why didn't you tell me?"

"You left that day before I even had a chance. And today I had other things on my mind, and my hands—" a wicked glint appeared in his eyes "—my hands were rather busy." As if his meaning wasn't clear enough, a large hand stole out to stroke the rounded flesh that peeped above the rumpled sheet.

Samantha's heart was suddenly so full she could hardly speak. "You bought this house . . . because of me? Jason . . ." Her hand touched his arm tentatively. "I wasn't expecting you to give up everything for me. I . . ." She took a deep breath, her eyes never leaving his. "I'd get used to living in Los Angeles."

"Samantha, this is your home." His quiet tone touched something inside her. "Your job is here. And as a writer, I'm flexible. I can work here as well as anywhere—better than anywhere since you're here."

"But your research . . ."

His lips touched hers lightly, possessively. "You're lucky enough to have an entire summer free. If we want to travel, fine. If not, then that's fine, too." He paused. "I've grown to like this little stretch of beach," he said lightly. "And the roof doesn't leak." His eyes caught and held hers before he grinned. "I could always use your house as an office."

Once again her heart began to sing. She climbed out of bed, dug in her purse for a second, and came up with a small rectangular object. The beautiful smile on her face deepened as she slipped beneath the sheets and dropped it into Jason's lap.

"I have a surprise for you, too."

"What's this?" He stared at the tiny package wrapped with a frilly red bow.

"You gave *me* Valentine's Day in June—now it's your turn."

"Well, I'll be damned—just like yours!" He grinned and held up a pair of men's jockey shorts. They were white and dotted with bright red hearts. "Where did you ever find these?"

"That's why I was so late getting here," she said dryly. "It wasn't easy trying to find a store that carried a gift like this during the summer."

"Think we'll ever wear them?"

She chuckled and ran her fingers down the length of one strong arm. "Not for long, I hope." A dimple appeared in one cheek. "My mother wants to know when the wedding is."

His hand closed over hers. His fingers circled the wedding finger of her left hand. "We could fly to Reno or Las Vegas tomorrow. Hell, why not tonight?"

Samantha laughed. "You *are* determined to make a gambling woman out of me yet. I think I should warn you, though, I only bet on a sure thing."

"Don't I know it!" he groaned, then his eyes darkened a little as they searched hers. "I can't promise you paradise, Samantha. I can only promise I'll love you for the rest of my life."

"Forever," she interrupted with a smile.

Jason relented with a kiss. "Forever," he murmured against her mouth.

"Jason." She frowned a little as her eyes searched his. "Are you really thinking of writing a thriller?"

"What!" Jason cocked a jaunty eyebrow. "Don't tell me you think I should stick with romances!"

"I can think of a few advantages," she admitted with a grin. "I wouldn't have to buy your books anymore." Her eyes gleamed as she ran her fingers tauntingly over the wiry curls covering his bare chest, pleased at the golden flame in his eyes, which flared brighter at the first faint brush of her fingers. "And it would be a shame to waste such talent. You really should do what you do best."

His eyes were alight with laughter as he looked at her. "Aren't you the woman who was my staunchest critic only a few weeks ago?"

She wrinkled her nose at him. "It's a woman's prerogative to change her mind. Although there is one drawback." Her eyes shone with love and laughter. "You'll be forever doomed to playing the role of the unsung hero!"

Jason's eyes wandered tenderly over her glowing face. "Oh, I think I'll learn to cope," he murmured warmly, "somehow." He bent his head to take her lips in a fiery kiss that spoke of the promise of the future...the promise of forever.

Take 4
Silhouette Special Edition novels
FREE...

and preview
future
books
in your
home for
15 days!

Start with 4 FREE books, yours to keep. Then preview 6 brand-new Special Edition® novels—delivered right to your door every month—as soon as they are published.

When you decide to keep them, pay just $1.9₂ each ($2.50 each in Canada), *with no shipping, handling, or other additional charges of any kind!*

Romance *is* alive, well and flourishing in the moving love stories presented by Silhouette Special Edition. They'll awaken your desires, enliven your senses, and leave you tingling all over with excitement. In each romance-filled story you'll live and breathe the emotions of love and the satisfaction of romance triumphant.

You won't want to miss a single one of the heartfelt stories presented by Silhouette Special Edition; and when you take advantage of this special offer, you won't have to.

You'll also receive a FREE subscription to the Silhouette Books Newsletter as long as you remain a member. Each lively issue is filled with news on upcoming titles, interviews with your favorite authors, even their favorite recipes.

To become a home subscriber and receive your first 4 books FREE, fill out and mail the coupon today!

Silhouette Special Edition®

Silhouette Desire

COMING NEXT MONTH

OUT OF THIS WORLD—Janet Joyce
When Adrienne met Kendrick, she thought he was an alien from outer space. He insisted he wasn't, but how could she believe him when his mere touch sent her soaring to the heavens?

DESPERADO—Doreen Owens Malek
Half Seminole Indian, Andrew Fox had chosen the dangerous life of a bounty hunter. As a student of Indian folklore, Cindy found him fascinating—as a woman, she found him irresistible.

PICTURE OF LOVE—Robin Elliott
It didn't take Steve long to realize Jade was the woman for him, but Jade was a compulsive overachiever. Could she manage to temper her ambition and make room for love?

SONGBIRD—Syrie A. Astrahan
Desirée had to choose—her career as a disk jockey in California or Kyle Harrison, the man she loved, in Seattle. Could she possibly find the best of both worlds?

BODY AND SOUL—Jennifer Greene
Joel Brannigan fought for what he wanted, and he wanted Dr. Claire Barrett. She was ready for a fair fight, but Joel didn't fight fair…and he always won.

IN THE PALM OF HER HAND—Dixie Browning
Fate had thrown Shea Bellwood and Dave Pendleton together under rather bizarre circumstances, but who can argue with fate—especially when it leads to love.

AVAILABLE NOW:

CAUTIOUS LOVER
Stephanie James

WHEN SNOW MEETS FIRE
Christine Flynn

HEAVEN ON EARTH
Sandra Kleinschmit

NO MAN'S KISSES
Nora Powers

THE SHADOW BETWEEN
Diana Stuart

NOTHING VENTURED
Suzanne Simms